"Try it on," Jager said.

Her fingers trembled. A small moth seemed to be fluttering in her throat. Paige let the dress drop back into the nest of tissue on the couch. "No," she said.

A frown appeared between his brows. "You don't like it? Black suits you. Believe me, you'll look great in that."

Paige knew she would. His instinct was unerring. In that dress she could be certain no one would be looking at her face.

She would look like his mistress.

Daphne Clair

HIS TROPHY MISTRESS

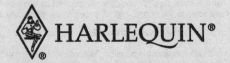

HARLEQUIN®

TORONTO • NEW YORK • LONDON
AMSTERDAM • PARIS • SYDNEY • HAMBURG
STOCKHOLM • ATHENS • TOKYO • MILAN • MADRID
PRAGUE • WARSAW • BUDAPEST • AUCKLAND

ISBN 0-373-12249-7

HIS TROPHY MISTRESS

First North American Publication 2002.

Copyright © 2001 by Daphne Clair De Jong.

CHAPTER ONE

THE bride and groom proceeded triumphantly down the aisle to the door of the church. Behind them Paige Camden, chief bridal attendant, kept her own smile in place and one eye on the five-year-old flower girl who seemed in danger of walking on the bride's white satin train.

Paige bent to place a restraining hand on the child's shoulder. As she straightened, casting an idle look at the nearer pews, her hazel eyes met a glittering jewel-green gaze that jerked her shoulders back and instantly eliminated her smile.

What the hell was Jager Jeffries doing at her sister's wedding?

And still as stunningly handsome as ever. Those astonishing eyes under well-defined brows contrasted with naturally olive skin; the stubborn masculine mouth and proud warrior's nose hinted at an unknown connection to some Maori ancestor.

The dark, luxuriantly waving hair was somewhat tamed by a surely expensive cut. An even more expensive suit hugged broad shoulders, tapered hips and long, muscular legs, its perfect fit and exquisite tailoring proclaiming how far the mature thirty-one-year-old had come from the wild young tearaway Paige had once known. And loved—with a passion so intense it was inevitably self-destructive, burning up in its own heat until only gray, dusty ashes remained.

"Paige?" The best man's hand was on her arm. "Are you okay?" he murmured, bending toward her.

The bridal party had forged ahead and guests were pressing from behind.

"Yes," Paige lied, resurrecting the smile. "I just stood on my dress, that's all."

She wrenched her gaze away from the piercing green one, unnecessarily shook out the violet floor-length skirt of her dress and stumbled forward, glad of the best man's supporting arm.

They reached the steps and the sunshine pouring out of a clear late-winter Auckland sky. A photographer motioned them into place beside the happy couple.

Paige kept the smile all through the photo session, and was still wearing it when they arrived at the crowded reception and she took her assigned place at the main table.

By that time her jaw was aching and her nerves humming like fine, overtensioned wires. When the best man poured her a glass of ruby-red wine she grabbed it with a shaking hand and downed half of it before she realized she'd spilled a drop on her satin gown.

Surreptitiously she dipped a corner of a linen table napkin into the crystal glass of iced water before her and dabbed at the stain. The wine color faded, and she rubbed the spreading watermark with the dry part of the napkin. At least at a distance it would be less noticeable than the wine.

She fixed a glazed stare on the table before her, telling herself it was imagination that she could feel Jager's gaze on her, that the hot prickling of sensation that assailed her skin was a by-product of long-buried memories that seeing him again had brought to the surface.

The succulent chicken and crisp salads on her plate might have been old rope and grass. She scarcely managed half a dozen mouthfuls, trusting the wine to stop them sticking in her throat.

Somehow she replied to her neighbors' efforts at conversation, and raised her glass and applauded the speeches at the right moments. And finally, despite her limited vision without her glasses, was unable to resist the urge to sweep her gaze about the red-carpeted, white-pillared reception lounge with its gilded decor and lavish floral arrangements, and find out if Jager really was there.

He was.

He sat at one of the nearer tables, leaning back in his half-turned chair and looking infuriatingly relaxed. As if he'd been waiting for her to find him, he lifted his glass to her in a mocking little gesture and drank, his eyes holding hers. Although the people around him were just a blur to Paige, and he was slightly out of focus, she felt the full force of his eyes.

Her hand tightened around her own glass, but she didn't return the silent toast, instead staring at him accusingly. *How dare you!* her eyes demanded. *How dare you turn up at Maddie's wedding and ruin the day for me?*

He must have been invited. Not by Maddie—her

sister would never have done that to her. So the invitation had come from Glen Provost, Maddie's new husband, or his family. How did he know Glen? Was Maddie aware of the connection, whatever it was? Why hadn't she warned Paige?

Jager replaced his glass on the white cloth. His long fingers twirled the fragile glass stem, and the corners of his mouth lifted in a faint smile while he continued to hold Paige's eyes.

Who was staring back at him, she realized, like a rabbit at a snake.

For the second time that day she dragged her gaze from him. She could feel the increased beat of her heart against the low-cut, fitted bodice of her dress, that seemed too tight. Drawing in a deep breath, she saw the best man's newly aroused interest in her bosom, his eyes first lingering, then in surprise flicking up to her face.

Not nearly as interesting, she mentally told him with grimly cynical humor. Her face would never be her fortune, not that she needed one, since she and Maddie were her father's only heirs.

There was nothing particularly wrong with ordinary hazel-green eyes, an unremarkable no-nonsense nose and a clear but hardly milk-and-roses complexion. They just didn't add up to the kind of eye-catching, man-snaring feminine prettiness that blessed her younger sister.

Maddie's eyes were blue and wide, her mouth a classic full-lipped bow, her nose cutely retroussé. And her hair was a tumble of blond natural curls that Paige would have killed for if she hadn't been so fond of her sister.

After years of trying to make hers curl, or fluff up, or even stay pinned in a style of any sort, Paige had despaired of persuading it to do anything but hang straight and fine, *au naturel.* Now she kept it neatly and boringly cropped to just below her ears, brushed it briskly to a satiny sheen every night, and after unsuccessfully experimenting with bleaches and rinses, allowed it to retain its own unexciting nut-brown color.

Long ago she had decided against competing with Maddie or any other pretty girl. Paige was plain and there was no point in pretending otherwise. She could just be thankful that she wasn't downright ugly, and that her figure as well as her face was passable, even if neither was likely to launch any ships. In fact her measurements were the same as her sister's, but Maddie had always seemed more rounded and ultra-feminine, perhaps because she was three inches shorter than Paige's five-eight.

Maddie had never had to worry that she was turning into a giraffe at age twelve. Their mother had never advised Maddie that makeup couldn't work miracles, and that discreetly enhancing her best features would be more effective than drawing attention to her face by using too much.

As the newlyweds cut the cake, Paige's mother put an elegantly slim, diamond-ringed hand on her waist and hissed in her ear, "What's Jager Jeffries doing here? Did you know he was coming?"

"No I didn't," Paige answered, scarcely moving her lips. "And I have no idea."

Margaret Camden's precisely reddened lips tightened. The blue eyes she had bequeathed to her younger daughter glittered with annoyance as she shook a head of artfully lightened curls. "I can't *believe* that Glen's family knows him!"

When the cake-cutting was completed and the bride and groom began circulating among the guests, Paige handed out wedding cake but stayed well away from the table where Jager sat, allowing the flower girl to deal with it. After returning the empty tray to the kitchen she retrieved her small makeup kit from her mother's handbag and crossed the carpeted lobby to the ladies' room.

She touched up the minimal color on her lips, checked that the subtle beige shadow on her eyelids was intact and the mascara that tipped her lashes hadn't run, and put on her large, rimless spectacles. Now that the photographs and the formal part of the wedding were over there was no reason she shouldn't wear them. It would have been nice to have contact lenses for occasions like this but, after painfully trying them several times in the past, Paige had accepted she was one of those people who just couldn't tolerate them.

Coming back into the lobby, she wished she had left the glasses in her bag. Because Jager stood only a few feet from the door, and without the slight, comforting vagueness that her impaired natural vision had imparted, he was very clearly, very solidly, in her way.

She knew, with a sense of inevitability, that he was waiting for her. That he'd followed her. A shimmer of pleased anticipation passed over her, and she firmly repressed it.

For a second or two neither of them moved. Paige searched Jager's face for some clue to his emotions, his intentions, but apart from the brilliance of his eyes he was giving nothing away.

Deciding to take the initiative, she ordered her lips to a smile—she'd had plenty of practice at that today—and said brightly, "Hello, Jager. This is a surprise! I didn't know you knew Glen."

"I don't," he answered, and at her flicker of surprise added, "not very well. It's a long story."

Which she didn't want to hear. "I'm sure it's an interesting one," she said, "but it will have to wait for another time."

Trying to look busy and purposeful, she attempted to pass him, but he reached out, closing his fingers around her arm. Her heart tripped over itself and her skin tingled.

"When?" His voice was low and gritty.

Something hot and disturbing happened in her midriff and began to spread throughout her body. Dismayed and disoriented by the force of it, she took a moment to make sure her voice was steady. "When what?"

"When can I see you?"

Warily she pulled away, and he let go. "Why do you want to see me?"

Thick black lashes momentarily hid his eyes. Then he looked away from her as if trying to distance himself. She saw the faint widening of his nostrils when he took a breath before looking back at her, his gaze curiously speculative. "To catch up," he said abruptly. "For old times' sake."

Two women and a man came out of the reception room, chatting and laughing as they headed for the rest rooms. Jager cast them an impatient glance and shifted so they could pass, his gaze homing in again on Paige.

"That's hardly necessary," she said.

"Necessary?" He pushed his hands into his pockets, looking down at her under half-closed lids from his six feet two inches. Dropping his voice to the deep purr that had always made her toes curl, he said, "It isn't necessary...but I'm curious. Aren't you?"

Intensely. But also cautious. Getting involved with Jager again was the last thing she needed right now. Ever. "No," she said baldly.

More people were trickling out of the lounge, some going outside, one group pausing to talk a few feet away. Jager ignored them. "Come on," he chided. "I thought your family was all keen on being tremendously civilized."

"Leave my family out of this!"

"Gladly." His beautiful lips curled.

She couldn't raise her voice here, but it trembled with anger. "I can't imagine why you'd want to talk—all we ever did at the end was argue."

Some spark of emotion lit his eyes, and a complicated expression crossed his face. "Not *all*," he reminded her. "There was always a way to end the argument." His lazy, explicit look invited her to remember...

Paige's lips compressed. Sweet, sweet memories—they had tormented her for years. "You said you wanted to talk!"

His head cocked, his expression becoming bland in the extreme. "Have I suggested anything else?"

He hadn't—not verbally. Paige felt wrong-footed, stuck for an answer.

Lights flickered on around them. In the big room the three-piece band her parents had hired struck up the wedding waltz.

"I have to go back," Paige said. "They're dancing."

Jager stood aside but she knew he was right behind her as she returned to the lounge.

The center of the floor had been cleared and Maddie and Glen were circling alone. A number of people had congregated near the doorway. Without pushing and causing a stir, Paige couldn't get through.

The music paused, and the Master of Ceremonies urged everyone onto the floor. Both sets of parents took up the invitation then, followed by several more couples.

The crowd at the door began to part, and Paige moved forward to skirt the edge of the dance floor.

An arm curved around her waist, urged her onto the polished boards.

"I can't..." she protested, but already her feet were following Jager's lead. "The best man...he'll be looking for me."

"He can find someone else," Jager said ruthlessly.

He took the makeup bag from her hand and dropped it onto the nearest table. "Dance with me, Paige."

He wasn't really giving her any choice unless she was to make a scene. He pulled her close, his other hand closing over hers and folding it against his chest. He'd opened his jacket and through the fine fabric of his white shirt she could feel the warmth of his skin, the faint beat of his heart. His scent enveloped her, familiar and strange at the same time.

A long time ago she had tried to teach him the proper steps that she'd learned at her exclusive girls' school, but he'd grinned and just held her and swayed to the music, scarcely moving his feet. Holding her close, body to body. Close enough for him to lay his cheek against her hair. Close enough to kiss.

Paige's eyes drifted shut. Memories washed over her and for just a few minutes she let them. She didn't speak and neither did Jager. She just breathed him in, his warmth, his personal male aroma, and remembered how it had been when they were young and in love, when she had believed they could overcome her parents' opposition, the differences in their backgrounds, lack of money, their own inexperience of life. Anything, so long as they had each other.

And of course like most young love it had come to nothing, all their dreams shattered into sharp, hurtful pieces against the cold, hard reality of the adult world.

She made a small sound—half sigh, half laugh— that should have been drowned by the music, and the chatter all around them, but Jager drew back a couple of inches and looked down at her. "What?" he queried.

A wry smile on her mouth, she said, "Nothing."

He continued to look at her, his gaze unreadable. "Nothing," he repeated. A gleam entered his half-closed eyes. "O-oh yeah?" For a moment his white teeth showed in a brief, blinding smile. Then his head went back and he laughed, a deeper, richer sound than she remembered from the days when he'd been scarcely more than a boy, but retaining the same uninhibited enjoyment.

Something caught at her throat, hot and thick, and an answering joyousness sang in her blood, a powerful echo of long-buried emotions.

Then he actually executed a few dance steps, quite expertly, taking her with him, holding her tight as she instinctively followed. She felt the power of his muscles as his thighs brushed against hers before he stopped, swinging her slightly off balance so she had to cling to his shoulder to stay upright.

They remained in an embrace that shut out everyone, everything. The laughter had left his face and he looked somber, the strong jaw clenched so that his beautiful mouth became uncompromising, his cheekbones more prominent. In the dark centers of his eyes Paige saw her own upturned face, and she was dimly aware that his hand had tightened on hers to the point of pain. Other sensations overrode the tiny hurt. Her breathing was shallow and quick, her throat tight, her body licked by a slow, languorous fire.

"Paige," he said, almost wonderingly, as if he'd just realized who it was he held.

Her lips parted hesitantly. His name hovered on them, then escaped like a sigh.

And another voice—her mother's, sharp and anxious—broke the moment. "Paige!"

She blinked at the interruption, instinctively trying to pull away from Jager, but he wasn't giving an inch.

Her mother stood within her father's arm. Henry appeared uncomfortable and annoyed, while his wife looked militant. "Blake is looking for you," she told Paige. "This should be his dance."

Blake? For a moment Paige's memory balked. The best man. "I didn't see him." She had seen no one but Jager since he'd swept her onto the dance floor. She looked up at him. "I'd better…" Again she tried to move away.

She recognized the quick jut of his jaw, the "don't push me" look in his eyes. But then he loosened his hold, dropping his hand from her tingling fingers although he still retained his grip on her waist, and allowed her to turn to her parents. Looking at them, he said politely, "How are you Mrs. Camden…Mr. Camden?"

Henry Camden nodded stiffly. Margaret said crisply, "We're well, Jager, and Paige…as you can see, she's fine." She paused, giving her daughter a covertly anxious glance before turning to him again. "We didn't expect to see you here."

"It was kind of a last-minute invitation."

"Really?" The chilly reply didn't encourage elaboration and he didn't offer it.

Henry's mature male rumble was directed at Jager. "I hear you've been doing very well for yourself."

Margaret looked at her husband in surprise. It was evidently the first she'd heard of it.

Jager said, "You do?"

"A bit of a highflier these days."

"I get by."

Henry gave a bark of reluctant laughter. "More than that, I'd say."

"Would you?"

Margaret demanded, "What are you talking about, Henry?"

Instead of explaining, Henry looked around them and said, "We're holding up the traffic here. If we're going to talk, we should move."

But the music stopped then, and other couples began walking off the floor.

Margaret shifted her gaze to Jager and said pointedly, "Paige has certain duties as her sister's attendant."

Jager inclined his head, and lifted both hands away from Paige. "I haven't balled and chained her." His eyes challenged her. His voice low, he asked, "Do you want to leave me, Paige?"

Echoes of the past rose, hauntingly. Had he meant to arouse them? "I do have things to do." She hated the apologetic note in her voice. Trying to sound more assertive she said, "It's been nice seeing you again, Jager."

Her mother looked relieved and approving. Jager merely lifted one dark brow a fraction and grinned at Paige. A tight, feral grin that both teased and promised, telling her she couldn't dismiss him so easily and it amused him that she'd even tried.

A shiver of apprehension spiraled about her spine. Jager had changed in the intervening years. For-

midably self-assured instead of cocky and defensive,
he carried a distinctly unsettling aura of sexual po-
tency that had little to do with the height and good
looks bequeathed by his unknown ancestors, and everything to do with how he saw himself as a man.
The raw, brash, quicksilver sexuality had been replaced by tempered steel under the polished surface
of a new sophistication. Which made him all the more
dangerous if, as she suspected, he had learned to use
it as a weapon.

Well, she had changed too, Paige told herself as
she left his side to hunt down either her sister or the
best man. She was no longer in thrall to teenage hor-
mones and romantic fantasies. There was more to love
than the seductive siren call of sex, more to life than
falling head over heels into lust and expecting it to
overcome all obstacles.

Paige no longer trusted feelings alone in her relationships. Having learned her lesson the hard way, she
had determined a long time back that for the rest of
her life her head would be the ruler of her heart.

She spied Maddie's veil enveloping blond curls,
and joined her sister, smiling at the people who had
engaged the bridal couple in talk. Maddie slid a
glance at her and gracefully extricated them both,
heading for the room set aside for the newlyweds to
change in later.

Closing the door, Maddie turned. "Are you all
right? I'm sorry, Peg." The childhood nickname
slipped out. "I had no idea Jager would turn up. It's
the most incredible coincidence—you wouldn't believe it!"

"Coincidence? Wasn't he invited?"

"Glen invited him. He didn't know…well, I've never mentioned Jager's actual name to him, so how could he? The thing is, Jager's kind of a long-lost relation."

"Of Glen's?"

Maddie nodded. "They're half brothers."

Paige's mouth fell open. Her thoughts whirled, and the one dazzling, golden one that surfaced and burst out into words was, "Jager found his family!"

Maddie was giving her a peculiar look.

Slowly the implications sank in. Paige gulped, swallowed and made a connection. "Glen's mother…?"

Her sister's white-veiled head shook vehemently. "His father…and some girl he knew before he got engaged to Glen's mother. Mrs. Provost doesn't know yet…with the wedding and everything it's not a good time for extra family stress. Mr. Provost asked the boys to keep it quiet until he gets around to telling her, but Glen wanted his new brother here for his wedding day. They've only met once or twice but they hit it off from the start, he said."

Glen was an only child; Paige could imagine he'd have been intrigued at the advent of an unknown sibling. "How long ago?" It must be recent.

"A few weeks, I think. Glen only told me today. I had no idea until then, and I couldn't get you alone before…I still haven't said anything to him about you and Jager." Maddie twisted her hands together. "Has it ruined the day for you?"

"Of course not!" It had been a stressful occasion

anyway, fraught with old pain and regrets, but she'd weathered it for Maddie's sake, and she would weather this too. No guilt and worry about Paige should be allowed to cloud Maddie's happy day. "Both of us have put our youthful indiscretion far, far behind us. It's quite fun," she lied gaily, "seeing him again, catching up on things."

His phrase, she realized, as Maddie looked doubtful, then relieved. "I guess it was all over years ago," Maddie said hopefully. "Are you sure you're okay with this?"

There wasn't much she—or anyone—could do about it. "I'm fine, stop worrying, Mad. Hadn't we better get back? Your husband will think you've left him already."

"Never!" Maddie turned to the mirrored dressing table and the makeup container sitting on it. "My husband," she repeated dreamily, fishing in the miniature hatbox and bringing out a lipstick. "Fancy me being an old married woman!" She began expertly applying the lipstick.

"Hardly old," Paige argued. Maddie was twenty-five to her own twenty-nine. "But old enough to know what you're doing, I guess. Which is more than I can say for my first venture into matrimony."

In the mirror, Maddie threw her a sympathetic look, shook out a tissue and blotted her lips. Gorgeous lips, Paige noted abstractly. Pink perfection. Glen was a lucky man. Her sister was as sweet as she was pretty, without a malicious bone in her body.

Scrunching the tissue, Maddie said, "It wasn't even

a proper wedding, was it? I mean, it hardly counts, really.''

"No." Paige's voice was perfectly steady. "It doesn't count at all."

CHAPTER TWO

JAGER didn't approach her again, but while Paige dutifully danced with the best man and then others, she was continually aware of him, leaning against a wall with arms folded or prowling the periphery of the room, exchanging a few words here and there with other guests, and for several minutes talking with Glen and Maddie.

When the bride and groom left, Paige kept her hands at her sides as Maddie tossed her bouquet into the crowd of well-wishers, allowing an excited young girl to catch it.

She was looking forward to slipping away now her duties were over. She couldn't have turned down Maddie's tentative request to attend her, hedged about with anxious assurances that Maddie would understand if she didn't want to. But now she felt drained and tired, with an incipient headache beating at her temples.

She sought out her mother and said quietly, ''Do you mind if I go on home now? I'm not needed anymore.''

''Of course, dear.'' Margaret searched her face. ''Your father and I have to stay until everyone's gone, but I'm sure Blake would drive you...'' Margaret looked around for the best man.

"No, give me my purse and I'll call a taxi. There's a phone in the lobby."

"Well...if you're sure."

"Yes. I'll see you in the morning." Paige leaned down and kissed her mother's cheek. "It was a lovely wedding."

"Yes, wasn't it?" Margaret glowed. At least this time she'd launched a daughter into matrimony in style.

In the lobby Paige found a card pinned above the phone with the number of a taxi company printed on it, and was dialing the final digit when a lean, strong hand came over her shoulder and pressed down the bar, leaving the dial tone humming in her ear.

"You don't need them," Jager's voice said. "I'll take you home."

Her hand tightened on the receiver. She didn't turn. "Thank you," she said, "but I'd prefer a cab."

"Why? My car's right outside."

Why? She couldn't think of an answer that didn't sound either unnecessarily rude or like an overreaction.

He lifted his hand and gently removed the receiver from her grasp, replacing it in the cradle. Belatedly she said, "I wouldn't want to take you out of your way..."

He didn't even bother to reply to that, already steering her toward the doors that swished open at their approach. "Where are you staying?"

"With my parents." She waited for some caustic remark, but all he said was, "The car's over here."

It was long and shiny, a dark navy-blue, she guessed, though it was difficult to tell at night.

The interior was spacious and the upholstery was real, soft leather.

Unless he was living beyond his means Jager had come up in the world. Her father had said something about him apparently doing well.

He slid into the seat beside her and buckled up his safety belt. When he turned the key in the ignition she scarcely heard the engine start, but they were soon gliding out of the car park.

"So," he said, "you came home for your sister's wedding. Last I heard you were living in New York."

"Yes." Paige shifted uneasily in the leather seat. "And you…? What are you doing now?"

He spared her a glance. "I run a telecommunications business, providing systems for industry."

"Is it a big business?"

"Big enough." He shrugged. "We're expanding all the time, increasing staff numbers."

"It sounds…interesting."

"It's challenging. New technologies are being invented and refined all the time. We have to stay a jump ahead, deciding which innovations are a flash in the pan and which will become industry standards."

"It sounds risky?"

"I've built a solid enough base that we can afford the odd risk. So far I haven't been wrong."

"You must be proud of yourself."

He seemed to ponder that. "Pride is what goes before a fall, isn't it?"

"Are you afraid of falling?"

He laughed, with that new, somehow disturbing male confidence. "Not anymore. Are you?"

She looked away from him, not answering.

He gave her a second or two, then said quite soberly, "I learned a long time ago, no matter how hard the fall, I can survive. And I never make the same mistake twice."

"It seems like a sound philosophy." She'd survived too. And she had no intention of scaling any heights again with him.

He said, "I heard you got married in America."

"Yes."

"Did your parents approve?"

"Yes, actually." They had come to the wedding, given their blessing.

"But you're alone now."

She didn't want his sympathy. Even less did she want to bare her feelings to him, of all people. To take the conversation away from herself she asked, "Are you married?"

The first question that had come to mind, but immediately she regretted asking. It could lead to a minefield.

"Like I said," he replied, "I never make the same mistake twice."

"Marriage isn't always a mistake," she said.

It left him an opening, she realized, and was thankful that he didn't take it. He gunned the motor and the car leaped forward before he lifted his foot slightly and the engine settled back into its subdued growl. When he spoke again his voice was remote and cool. "I suppose you can't wait to get back to…America."

Evasively she answered, "I'll be spending some time with my family."

"How much time…days, weeks?" He paused. "Months?"

"I'm not sure."

He flashed a glance at her. "He must be pretty accommodating…your husband."

Her thoughts skittering, she realized Jager didn't know…

Why should he? Her mouth dried, and her throat ached. She stared through the windscreen with wide-open eyes until they stung and she had to blink. "My husband—"

She didn't see the other car until it was right in front of them—it seemed to have come from no-where, the headlights blinding, so close that her voice broke off in a choked scream and she raised her arms before her face, knowing that despite Jager's frantic wrench at the wheel, accompanied by a sharp, shock-ing expletive, there was no way he could avoid a col-lision.

A horrified sense of inevitability mixed with cold, stark terror, and the awareness that maybe this was how—and when—she was going to die.

With Jager, said a clear inner voice, and the thought carried with it both tearing grief and a strange, fleeting sensation of gladness.

The heavy thump and screech of metal on metal filled her ears and the impact jolted her against the seat belt. She was vaguely aware of the windscreen, glimpsed between her shielding arms, going white and opaque, then it disappeared and the two cars, locked together, slid across the road in a slow, agonizing waltz until they came to a jarring halt against a building.

Daring to lower her arms, Paige heard Jager's voice, seemingly somewhere in the far distance. "Paige—*Paige!* Are you all right?"

His hand gripped her shoulder, and by the light of a street lamp she saw his face, a deathly color, with dark thin trickles of moisture running from his forehead, his cheeks and his eyes blazing.

"You're bleeding," she said, raising an unsteady hand to touch one of the small rivulets, wanting suddenly to cry. She couldn't bear the thought of him being disfigured.

"Never mind that," he said impatiently. "Are you hurt?" His hands slid from her shoulders down her arms, and he swore vehemently. "You're bleeding too."

She was, from several tiny glass nicks on her bare forearms. "It's nothing." She moved her legs, found them whole and unhurt. "I'm all right. Are you?"

"Nothing broken."

In the background someone was yelling. Car doors slammed and then a face peered into the space left by the broken windscreen. "The police and ambulance are on their way," said a male voice. "Anyone hurt in there?"

"We're okay," Jager answered. "Can you get the passenger door open? My side's too badly damaged."

* * *

Ambulance staff checked them both and told them they were lucky, but to contact an emergency medical service if they experienced delayed symptoms.

The other driver, miraculously walking, though groggy and with a broken arm, was taken to hospital. While the police were noncommittal when they breath-tested Jager and took statements from both him and Paige, it was fairly obvious the injured man had been drinking.

Within half an hour the cars had been dragged away and the police offered to take Paige and Jager home.

Jager gave them Paige's parents' address and climbed into the car beside her. He handed her purse to her and she realized he'd retrieved it from the wreckage.

When the car drew up outside the house he got out and helped her to the pavement, and said to the driver, "Thanks a lot. We appreciate the lift."

He had his arm around her and was urging her to the gateway as the police car pulled away from the kerb.

"Don't you want them to take you home?" she said. "You don't need to come in with me."

"It doesn't look like your parents are in yet. I'm not leaving you alone."

The garden lights were on—they were on an automatic timer—but the house was in darkness.

When she drew out the key Jager took it from her and opened the door, closing it behind them as he accompanied her into the wide entryway. He found the light switch and she said, "The burglar alarm. You have to press that yellow button on the key-tag."

He found it and then handed the key on its electronic tag back to her. She felt a trickle of moisture on her forehead and lifted a hand to find the source, wincing as her fingers encountered something sharp. She stared at the tiny droplet of blood on her finger. "I've got glass in my hair."

Jager had regained some of his normal color, but his eyes were darkened in the center, the irises now more gray than green, his mouth tight as he surveyed her. "We need a bathroom," he said, "to clean up."

There was one off her room, shared with the bedroom that had been her sister's when they both lived at home. "Come upstairs," she offered. It was the least she could do.

Jager's face was streaked with blood too, and there were red spots on his shirt. His hair was ruffled out of its sleek styling, speckled with sparkling fragments of glass.

He followed her up the wide marble staircase, carpeted in the middle so that their footsteps were silent.

The door to her room was open. Paige swiftly crossed to the bathroom, switching on the light. White and merciless, it shone on shiny decorative tiles and a glass-enclosed shower, bold gold-plated taps and big fluffy towels.

She took a towel and facecloth from a pile on a shelf, handing a set to Jager. "You'd better wash your face."

While he did so she opened one of the mirrored

cupboards, grimacing at her pale reflection, with a smear of blood across the forehead.

As Jager dried himself she turned with a comb in her hand, holding it out to him. "Wait. I'll get something to catch the glass." If they used one of the towels the slivers would be caught in the pile.

In the bedroom she removed a pillowcase, leaving the covers rumpled, and hurried back to spread it on the bathroom floor. "Now you can comb the glass out of your hair."

"You first." He reached out, lifted her spectacles from her nose and placed them on the marble counter. Before she could protest his hand curled around her nape, warm and compelling.

"I can do my own."

"You can't see it," he replied calmly. "Bend forward a bit, honey. You don't want glass down your cleavage."

The casual endearment had caught her unawares, sending a soft warmth through her. Afraid he'd read the heat in her cheeks, and maybe something in her eyes that she didn't want him to see, she bowed her head.

His fingers slid gently through her hair from nape to crown, followed by the stroke of the comb. Fragments of glass made a tiny pattering on the pillowcase. He combed carefully though the fine strands, then gave a muttered exclamation, and she felt a prickle of pain.

"This might hurt," he said tersely. She held her breath, and bit her lip against a sudden sting.

"There." He dropped a bloodied sliver on the pillowcase. "It was embedded, but I think I've got it all. Don't move."

He grabbed a facecloth and ran cold water on it, then she felt the coolness pressed to the place where the glass had pierced the skin. "It's bleeding a bit," he said, "but it wasn't deep."

"You're bleeding more than I am." He'd taken the full force of the shattered windscreen, too busy fighting for both their lives to even try to protect himself as she had done.

"It's nothing. Just a few nicks." He lifted the cloth. "That's better. Do you have some disinfectant?"

"Not necessary." She lifted her head. "I'm fine, really."

"Really." He sounded as if he didn't believe her. His free hand caught her chin, a frown of concentration on his brow. "You didn't get any in your face."

"No." She stepped back, but now he took her hand, and led her to the wide basin. "We haven't finished yet." He put in the plug and turned on a tap with one hand, still holding her in a firm grip with the other.

"Look, I—"

"Shh," he admonished. "Hold still."

He gently wiped the remaining blood from her forehead and bathed her arms, washing away the red streaks, leaving only tiny puncture wounds. "You were lucky," he said. "We both were."

The water had turned pale pink and he let it out, reached for one of the towels and patted her skin dry. "You'll want to change." He was eyeing her ruined dress—streaked with blood, and torn where she'd caught it on something as they were helped out of the car.

Paige recalled worrying about the wine stain, seemingly aeons ago, and thought how little it mattered. They might both have been killed.

She shivered, remembering the horrible, stark fear of those few moments when the world seemed about to end for her. And for Jager.

His hands closed over her arms. "It's all right. You're all right."

"I know." But her voice was unsteady and she couldn't stop trembling. She supposed shock was setting in.

Jager drew her toward him, but then he stopped and cursed under his breath, looking down at his bloodied clothes. "Can you get out of that dress by yourself?" he asked her.

Paige nodded jerkily. But she didn't move, and the tremors that racked her were getting worse.

"Here." He turned her, and she felt the zipper at the back of the ruined dress being opened, all the way to the end of her spine. Then the dress was lifted away from her shoulders and it slithered to her feet, leaving her in a mauve half-cup bra, matching bikini briefs and a pair of lace-topped stockings that were snagged and laddered.

"Step out of it," Jager said.

Like an automaton she obeyed, lifting one foot from the tangled satin of the dress. Her shoe caught in the folds and she lost her balance, kicking off the other shoe in an effort to regain it.

Jager's hands closed about her arms, swung her around to face him, and her hand momentarily flattened against his chest.

Her startled eyes met his, and her trembling abruptly stopped.

The particles of glass caught in the blackness of his hair sparkled like a scattering of diamonds, and his eyes had the sheen of polished jade. The flawless male skin was marked by small wounds, one trickling a thin line of blood onto his cheekbone.

Unconsciously Paige touched her tongue to her upper lip, bringing Jager's gaze to her mouth. Another tremor shook her body, and his head jerked up a fraction. His hands tightened but he kept the few inches space between them. "Have you got something warm to put on?" he asked her, his voice low and rough.

Paige blinked, nodded.

"Then go and do it," he ordered. "I'll clean up in here." He gave her a little push. "Go on."

She did, dragging a thick terry-cloth robe from her wardrobe. When Jager pulled the bathroom door wide and entered the bedroom she was tying the sash at her waist, clumsily because her hands were shaking. Her torn stockings lay on the bed.

The light no longer picked up glints from his hair. He must have combed out the glass. And he'd taken off his jacket—and his shirt. To wash out the bloodstains, she supposed. "I tossed the glass in the waste bin," he said. "And the pillowcase into the clothes basket. What do you want to do with this?" He had her dress in his hands.

"Leave it." She was trying to be calm and controlled, but little shivers kept attacking her in waves. Despite the heavy toweling wrap she felt cold. Her gaze went to the dress in his hands. "I'll have to throw it out."

A faint, knowing contempt touched his mouth, and she said defensively, "It's ruined." It might be a waste but the dress was beyond repair.

He looked down at the crushed and stained fabric. "Pity. You looked marvelous in it."

He began folding it, clumsy but careful.

She had never looked *marvelous* in anything. She'd looked good in it, Paige knew—as good as she ever would. But it was silly to feel a pleased glow at the compliment.

The shiny fabric slipped in his hands, his attempt at folding coming to grief.

"It doesn't matter," Paige said, unaccountably irritated. "Give it to me."

She crossed to him and took the dress from him and into the bathroom, where she shoved the thing willy-nilly into the rubbish container in the corner, slamming the lid back on.

Jager's shirt was spread across the heated towel rail, damp in patches. She couldn't see his jacket, and supposed he'd hung it on the hook behind the door.

When she turned he was standing in the doorway, watching her.

Defensively she folded her arms across herself as she made her way back into the bedroom. Jager stood aside but as she passed him she caught a whiff of his skin-scent, bringing back unbearably powerful, poignant memories. Warm nights and a warm bed, and

Jager's warm raw-silk nakedness under her hands, against her own heated skin...

Hurriedly she moved away from him, and turned to find him looking at the ruined stockings lying on the bed, but then he lifted his eyes and they seemed to be searching for something in hers.

She should look away. Instead she found her gaze wandering to his mouth, a mouth made for temptation, for seduction. A mouth that could wreak magic on a woman's body. And his broad chest, a masculine perfection where her hands had once roamed at will, where she'd lain her cheek against his heart after making love. Her eyes reached the discreet silver buckle of the belt that snugged his dark trousers to his slim waist, and her heartbeat quickened.

She didn't have her glasses on, she reminded herself. Any flaws would be mercifully invisible to her. No man could possibly look as good as Jager did right now.

"Enjoying yourself?"

His voice brought her back with a start to what she was doing.

She tried to brazen it out. "Just checking. I would have thought you'd at least have bruises."

He flexed his right shoulder and shifted his leg, apparently testing. "I may have, tomorrow." He grimaced.

"You *were* hurt! Why didn't you tell the ambulance officers?"

"It's nothing. They gave me a pretty thorough going-over."

"They're not doctors."

"I'm fine." He swung the arm to show her. "See?"

Unconvinced, but conscious of how much worse it might have been, she shivered again. "You might have been killed."

"So might you." He looked grim suddenly. "You're still cold. Maybe you should have a warm shower and get into bed."

"With you here?"

"I won't join you—unless I'm invited."

"You're not invited!"

He folded his arms across that splendid chest, and looked regretful. "I thought not. But don't let me stop you." As she hesitated, he said, "This is no time to be prudish, Paige. It'll be at least fifteen minutes before my shirt is dry. You might as well use the time— unless you'd rather spend it talking to me."

No, she wouldn't...would she? Paige plumped for the lesser evil. "All right," she mumbled, and made for the bathroom.

The shower felt good. Wincing at the tender spot where Jager had dug glass from her scalp, she washed her hair. Five minutes with the hair dryer left it shining and soft, and she put her undies into the clothes basket and pulled the terry gown back on, because she hadn't thought to bring anything else into the bathroom with her.

She fingered Jager's shirt and lifted it from the towel rail, switched on the hair dryer again to play it over the remaining dampness, then returned to the bedroom with the shirt in her hand. "It's dry," she told him.

"Thanks." He'd been lounging on the bed, his head propped on the pillows. The sight gave her a start; he looked so much at home, as if he belonged there.

He stood up and stretched out his hand for the shirt, but then, as if he couldn't help it, his hand bypassed the shirt and touched her hair, stroked its newly washed sleekness, and his thumb traced the outline of her ear.

Paige's heart stopped. She forgot to breathe. Couldn't speak. Her eyelids fell of their own accord, before she jerked them open. "What are you doing?"

His hand had come to a stop, a hank of her hair trapped in his fist. "Where's your husband?" His voice was deep and indistinct, and his jewel-eyes glittered into hers. "Damn him, why isn't he here looking after you?"

The unexpected question widened her eyes, and her lips parted on a caught breath. Obscure anger shook her. "I'm a grown woman, Jager. I don't need a man to *look after* me." Never mind that Jager had done just that tonight, very competently, for which until this moment she'd been grateful. "And as for my husband," she added huskily, and took a deep breath, "he…Aidan's…"

"Not here," Jager said harshly. And then his other arm came around her body, crushing her against him, and his mouth on hers smothered the words she was trying to say, sent her thoughts spinning into deep space and made her forget everything except his kiss.

CHAPTER THREE

IT WAS a kiss that took her breath, her heart, her soul. She couldn't think, couldn't move, except to lift her arms and cling, as if she were drowning in the wine-dark sea of desire and he was her only hope of survival.

The blood running through her veins sang his name, her skin was licked by fire, her limbs turned to liquid flame. The taste of him was an intoxication, the hard length of his body against hers a ravishment.

She opened her mouth to him and he took swift advantage of the invitation, making the kiss deeper, unashamedly sensual, a merciless invasion of her senses.

His hand pushed aside the front of her robe and settled on her breast, his thumb and forefinger finding the budding center, making her moan with ecstasy and arch herself against him, triumphant when she recognized the thrust of his arousal pressing at the apex of her thighs.

She brought one hand down to his bared chest in imitation of his caress, reveling in the heat and slight dampness of his skin against her palm, once as familiar to her as her own body.

Then his mouth left hers and his arms lowered, lifting her. She gasped, clutching at his shoulders, and his lips closed over her breast. With an inarticulate cry of pleasure, she let her head fall back. Dizzy and disoriented, she was wholly given over to sensation.

She hardly realized he had swung them round until his mouth momentarily left her and they fell together onto the bed. Before she'd drawn breath he impatiently untied the belt of her robe and bared her body to his hot, questing gaze. She stared back at him boldly as his hands traversed her from neck to knee, rediscovering the shape of her breasts, her hips, her thighs. There was color on his lean cheekbones, and his fingers were unsteady, his eyes heavy-lidded and glowing with desire. That look had always filled her with wonder—wonder that *she* could do this to him. That he wanted her so much.

One hand slipped between her thighs, and the other left her to undo his belt. He stroked her softly until she was wild with need, then stood for a few seconds to shuck the remainder of his clothing and sheath himself. Watching, she was briefly thankful that he'd thought of it, then he was beside her, taking her again into his arms, answering her frantic, silent plea to let her take him in, to experience the whole of him, and at last, without equivocation or delay, filling her with himself, driving her to the pinnacle and beyond, to that nameless place where past and present and future didn't exist, but only the blinding, transcendental moment.

While the world drifted back into focus Paige resisted opening her eyes. Her cheek rested on Jager's shoulder, and her legs were still tangled with his, his arm warm around her.

He moved, and she held her breath, afraid he would

leave, but he only settled closer, enfolding her again. He kissed her closed eyelids, then feathered more tiny kisses along her cheek, and down her neck to her shoulder. She smiled, and he kissed her lips, long and tenderly, with an underlying hint of passion. Against her mouth, he murmured, "Tissues?"

Paige gave a little laugh, and reached without looking for the drawer of the bedside table.

Eventually she had to open her eyes. Jager was on his way to the bathroom, giving her a heart stopping view of his naked back, but in minutes he returned. She said sleepily, "Turn off the light."

He detoured to do it, then came back to her, drawing her again into his arms and pulling a sheet over them both. "That was to dream of," he said. "But too damn quick."

His palm spanning her belly, he teased her navel with his thumb, while his lips wandered along her shoulder, nuzzling and nibbling. Her eyelids fluttered down, and a deliciously lethargic pleasure rippled all the way to her toes. As Jager's hands and his mouth pleasured and tantalized, she moved her body subtly under his ministrations, allowing him better access there, hinting that some attention would be appreciated here.

He had always been good at this, she thought, a hint of sadness penetrating the dreamy aura he was creating. A silent tear trembled at the corner of her eye and coursed into her hair.

Jager found the salty track with his lips, and murmured, "What? Crying?"

"No," she denied, not wanting to think about what

had been or what might have been, or what might still be. She turned her head and met his lips with hers, aligned her body with his, thrust her knee between his thighs, to blot out the thoughts, the memories.

Jager responded with a surge of passion, and when she opened herself to him again and welcomed him with a sigh of satisfaction, he came to her as deeply and completely as before, but until the moment when he shuddered uncontrollably against her, a muffled sound tearing from his throat, there was gentleness in him this time, a tender concern in his touch.

Afterward he didn't leave her side, holding her close in his arms until she drifted into an exhausted, velvety sleep. Her last thought was that he'd be gone by morning, and her heart gave a small throbbing ache at the prospect.

When she woke a weak morning sun was streaming though the window. Jager, fully dressed but without tie or jacket, leaned on the window frame, watching her.

"Oh, God!" She closed her eyes again, hoping he was a figment of her imagination. Or perhaps she was still dreaming.

"I didn't think I looked that bad," he said.

Paige opened her eyes again. He was fingering his chin, his eyes both wary and amused. He'd shaved, and his hair was damp and sleek. He must have used her bathroom, borrowed a razor, and she hadn't heard a thing. "You've been here all night?" she said.

A dark brow rose. "You don't remember? I'm disappointed. Shall I tell you what we did?"

"I know what we did!" Foolishly, she felt her cheeks burn. "I thought you'd leave before...now."

"You mean before your parents find out I'm here."

Paige clamped her lips. It was what she'd meant. No point in restating the obvious.

Vaguely she recalled hearing a car, the sounds of her parents' return, but she wasn't sure when. She'd been too engrossed in Jager, in the pleasure he was giving her, to even care.

She felt at a distinct disadvantage, lying naked in bed while he stood there patently at ease, his arms loosely folded. Clutching at the sheet for modesty, she sat up and looked around for something to put on.

Jager moved, a little awkwardly, stooping to pick up the toweling robe from the floor. "Is this what you want?"

"Thank you." She had to drop the sheet to take it and pull it on, and he didn't turn away.

Kicking away the bedclothes, she swung her feet to the floor, belting the robe. When she stood up he was close by, only a foot or two from the bed, his hands now thrust into the pockets of his trousers. "You should have told me if you wanted me to leave," he said.

"Would you have?"

"What the lady wants, the lady gets." The mockery in his voice reminded her that last night she'd wanted *him*—desperately, recklessly. Without any thought of consequences and repercussions.

Well, this was what she'd got. She looked at the clock. She could hear sounds of stirring in the house. There was little hope of spiriting Jager out without being seen. Being caught trying would be more embarrassing than fronting up about his presence.

Maybe reading her thoughts, he said, "I could climb out the window, but the neighbors might notice."

Paige said stiffly, "If you wait until I'm dressed, we'll go downstairs and I'll explain we were involved in an accident and you were slightly injured so…as my sister's room was free, you stayed overnight."

Momentarily his jaw tightened. "And I'm supposed to go along with that?"

Her gaze fell away as she said, "I hope you will."

"I don't suppose they'll swallow it." He paused. "Will they tell your husband? Will *you?*"

Her eyes swung back to him, wide with shock.

"What sort of man is he?" Jager queried harshly. "If he hurts you…" His hands clenched into fists, and his expression turned dangerous.

Paige took a moment to orient herself. "Do you think I'd have slept with you if…?" Stopping short, she swallowed and took a deep, sustaining breath. "You have no idea," she said, gathering dignity to herself like a shield, "what you're talking about. My husband died six months ago."

For once she saw Jager rocked off balance. His expression went totally blank, his cheeks almost colorless. The firm, stubborn chin jerked up as if he'd been hit, and his body seemed to go rigid.

Before he could pull himself together, she'd marched across the carpet into the bathroom, locking the door behind her.

*   *   *

When she came out Jager had recovered his equilibrium, although he looked a trifle paler than usual. His eyes were shuttered, with the watchful, not-giving-anything-away look that he'd worn for much of the previous day. He had taken up a stance near the door to the passageway, his back to the frame, hands in his pockets.

"Why didn't you tell me before?" he asked her.

Paige was opening a drawer to pull out undies. "I was trying to when we crashed. When I realized you didn't know." She went to the built-in wardrobe and opened the double doors. They made an effective screen as she blindly reached for a pair of jeans and hauled them on.

"You didn't say anything last night…here."

Paige found a sweater and pulled it over her head. What was she supposed to have done? Paused in the middle of that mind-blowing lovemaking and said, *By the way, did you know my husband died?*

She adjusted the sweater over her hips. "The subject didn't come up."

Stepping out of the screening doors, she closed them with a snap. When she went to the dressing table she could see Jager behind her and to one side. She picked up a hairbrush and flicked it cursorily over her hair. Last night she'd omitted the customary fifty strokes, but with him watching she wasn't inclined to make up for it now.

"We might as well go down," she said, replacing the brush.

"And get it over with?"

Paige shrugged, on her way to the door.

His hand on the knob, Jager said, "I should say I'm sorry about your husband."

That was an odd way of putting it, but he looked sober, even genuinely sympathetic. She nodded. "Thank you."

For a long moment he stood just looking at her, his gaze probing and perhaps puzzled. Then he opened the door and waited for her to precede him.

Their appearing together in the breakfast room caused a distinct shock to her parents, but on the face of it they seemed to accept Paige's explanation. At the mention of an accident her mother was more concerned with any likely injuries than where—or how—Jager had spent the night. She peered at Paige's face anxiously. "You might have been scarred!"

"I'm not," Paige pointed out. "We were lucky."

She invited Jager to sit at the table, and offered him toast and coffee. Her mother, after a minute or two, switched to hostess mode and asked if he'd like bacon and eggs.

"No, thanks," he answered. "Coffee and toast is fine."

Her father turned to Jager. "You hurt your leg?" he asked gruffly.

Jager had come down behind Paige and she hadn't noticed anything wrong. She looked at him. Was it an act to back up her story?

"Nothing's broken," Jager answered her father, just as he'd told her. "I'm a bit stiff after last night." He glanced at Paige, and she looked hastily away. "I seem to have muscles I never knew about."

"What about you, Paige?" Henry asked. "Perhaps we should take you to a doctor just in case."

"I'm all right. The impact was mostly on the driver's side."

Jager had made sure of that, turning the wheel as far as he could before the other car hit. Startled by the thought, she looked at him. "Were you trying to save me?"

He looked back at her for a moment, then shrugged. "I was trying to save us both. Instinct took over."

An instinct that put him directly into the path of an oncoming car? Paige curled her hand around the cup of coffee she'd poured for herself. He'd have done it for anyone, she guessed. Any woman, at least. A natural male reaction maybe, latent even in twenty-first century man.

"I'm grateful anyway."

Her mother said, "I'm sure we all are."

Jager's mouth twitched at the corners as he turned to Margaret. "Thank you, but I don't need gratitude, Mrs. Camden." His tone, although perfectly courteous, implied he didn't need anything—not from her nor her husband. "And Paige has already shown hers." His eyes sought her apprehensive gaze and he continued smoothly, "She patched up my wounds, such as they were, and insisted I stay the night."

Margaret's eyes too went to her daughter. Paige avoided her gaze, reaching for marmalade that she didn't need. "The cuts looked worse than they were," she said. "I'll wash the things from the bathroom later. And the sheets from Maddie's room." She didn't want her mother or the cleaning woman who would come tomorrow noticing that Maddie's bed hadn't been slept in. And she'd certainly be washing the sheets from her own bed.

Paige had little appetite, and Jager ate quickly and sparingly before pushing back his chair. After thanking Margaret he said, "I'll collect my things from…upstairs and be on my way."

Paige rose too, noticing that he winced as he stood up, his grip on the chair back turning his knuckles momentarily white.

He was limping as they left the room, and he gripped the banister all the way up the stairs.

In the bathroom he picked up his jacket and tie, then came back to her room. "Thanks," he said, "for everything."

"I could borrow a car and run you home."

He seemed to be trying to read her expression before shaking his head. "I'll call a cab."

"If you like."

They were standing feet apart, and it seemed he was as tongue-tied as she.

Then he moved, came close and lifted her chin with his big, capable hand. "What was it about—last night—Paige? For you?"

Paige struggled for words. It had been unexpected, out of character and, in the light of day, inappropriate.

But fantastic, an inner voice reminded her.

Trying to ignore that, she said huskily, "I don't know. I suppose…reaction to the accident." She'd heard danger was an aphrodisiac, but had always found the theory difficult to believe. Maybe there was something in it after all. "And," she added, determined not to flinch from the truth, "it's some time since I...since I had sex."

His eyes narrowed, so that she couldn't read their expression. "Since you were widowed?"

The brutal question stiffened her spine, and she stepped back, away from his light grasp. "Yes," she said harshly. "If you must know." Surely he didn't think she made a habit of one-night stands?

"And before that," Jager's voice was soft, "did your husband fulfill your needs?"

"Yes!" she shot at him, and then firmly clamped her mouth. She wouldn't discuss Aidan with him. And her sexual needs were her own business.

His mouth too had tightened, to an ominous line. What did he want, a confession that he was king in the bedroom? He wouldn't get it from her.

"So," he said, "where do we go from here?"

Be strong, she exhorted herself. We've been down that road once and it only leads to heartache. Heartache and emptiness. "We're not going anywhere, Jager. Last night was...nice..."

"Nice!"

"...but it doesn't mean we have any kind of...relationship."

"We have a relationship," he argued, "whether you like it or not. Whether your family likes it or not."

"Had," she insisted. "Past tense."

"You know that's not true!"

Rallying herself, she argued, "It's true for me. I've

moved on, and I don't want to go back. Whatever we had in the beginning didn't last long, did it?''

''It might have if—''

Paige said sharply, ''Better not to go there, surely. We'll only start fighting again, and I don't want that.''

''Neither do I.''

''Then leave it, Jager…please? Last night…maybe it was a mistake, but let's not spoil the memory by parting in anger.''

He looked belligerent and frustrated, but finally nodded curtly. ''All right. You've made your point. You won't object to one goodbye kiss?''

Without giving her a chance to do so, he crossed the space between them and took her shoulders in his hands, bending his head to part her lips with his mouth.

Paige tried to remain unmoved, but the persuasion of his mouth moving across hers softened her resistance, and although she somehow kept her hands clenched at her sides her mouth gave him back kiss for kiss.

Then she was free. Jager gave her a hard look, nodded briefly as if satisfied, and turned to limp to the door.

Trailing after him, she felt uneasy despite his apparent capitulation, and there was a hollow feeling in her midriff that threatened to turn into panic.

She had done the right thing, she assured herself when his cab had collected him. There was no future for her with Jager. Once bitten was enough.

Turning her mind to practicalities, she hurried upstairs and stripped the beds in both bedrooms, bundled up the sheets with the used towels and cloths from the bathroom and took them down to the laundry.

Her mother found her sprinkling washing powder into the machine. "Paige? What on *earth* were you thinking of? I'd have thought you'd have more sense than to let that young man drive you home. And as for inviting him to stay...! I suppose he'd been drinking."

An emotion familiar from long ago made Paige clench her teeth. Busying herself with the control panel she said, "He offered me a ride and it seemed silly to refuse. The accident wasn't his fault, Mother. I suppose he'd have had a glass or two of wine at the reception, but he was under the limit when the police tested him. And he probably saved my life—or at least saved me from being injured."

"You're defending him again," Margaret accused shrilly. "Just as you always did."

"I'm trying to be fair." Jager didn't need her to defend him—he never had. She'd expended a lot of energy doing it nevertheless, and alienated herself from her family. She didn't want that to happen again. "Don't worry, I won't be seeing him anymore."

Relief flooded Margaret's face. "I'm so glad to hear that, darling!" She stepped forward to put her arms around her daughter. "He was never suitable for you, you know that."

"Yes," Paige said dully. "I know."

She did know. Her parents had been right all along, so why did the words make her feel like a traitor?

* * *

The following day while she was helping her mother pack some wedding presents that had been sent to the house, ready for the honeymooners' return, the phone rang and the cleaning woman called her.

Picking up in the spacious foyer, she wished she'd chosen a less public extension when Jager's voice answered her brief hello with a simple, spine-tingling, "Paige."

Her breath momentarily stopped. She found herself looking about furtively for anyone within earshot, but the cleaning woman had disappeared and her mother was still busy with wrappers and boxes in another room. "What do you want?"

For a second he didn't reply. When he did there was a subtle change in his tone. "That's a leading question."

"It wasn't meant to be." Remembering his limp yesterday, she said, "Are you all right?"

"Yes. What about you?"

"Perfectly. Is that why you rang?"

"Not the only reason. What are you doing tonight?"

"Nothing—I mean, nothing that involves you."

He gave a short laugh. "That's blunt."

"I'm sorry."

"Are you? Then why cut off your nose to spite your face—or is it to keep the peace with your family?"

"I don't think there's any point in raking over old...embers."

"They were more than embers the other night."

Paige bit her lip as a warm tide of remembrance

washed over her. "It didn't mean anything—if we hadn't both been reacting to the shock of nearly being killed it would never have happened."

"Not then, maybe..."

"Not ever. And it will never happen again."

"If I were a betting man..."

She knew she'd made a mistake. Jager could never resist a challenge. "Jager," she said, closing her eyes tightly. "Don't. It's only six months since I lost my husband. Maddie's wedding was a bit of a strain, then with the accident coming on top of it...I guess I wasn't thinking straight."

"And now you're regretting it." His voice had hardened.

Obviously he didn't share her regret. "It didn't mean anything! So please, leave it at that."

"What if I can't?"

"It takes two," she argued. "And I hope you'll respect my feelings."

"I respect your feelings," he said. "Why don't you?"

"What do you mean?"

"Think about it," he advised dryly, "and let me know when you've sorted them out."

She heard the gentle click in her ear with a mixture of anger and relief. Let him know when she'd sorted out her feelings? Hell would freeze while he waited.

When she had allowed Jager to believe she would be returning to America, Paige had been less than frank. She had come home prepared to review her future and start a new chapter in her life. And grateful for the support of her family.

By the time Maddie and Glen returned from their honeymoon, Paige had a job doing graphic design in a large printing firm, and she'd bought a cottage perched on the edge of the inner harbor. The back of the house gave a view of the water through native trees growing on a steep slope.

"Mother thinks you're nuts," Maddie told her candidly the first time she and Glen visited, finding Paige scraping flaky paint from a window frame. "She expected you to get a place in the city. Something low maintenance and—well, not like this."

"So did I, really."

She had only looked at this place because of its location. When the estate agent told her he had an old cottage on a neglected section with native bush and a sea boundary, she'd envisaged demolishing it and putting up a new home to her own design, but something about the shabby, sleepy-looking cottage appealed to her, and impulsively she'd decided instead to rescue it.

Glen surveyed the tired paint and sagging porch. "It'll take more than a lick of paint to fix this up."

Reluctantly Paige put down the scraper. "Can I make you two a cuppa?"

Inside, Glen looked around the small, dark living room and scuffed his toe on its worn carpet. "I bet there's kauri under that. Or rimu, maybe."

There probably was. Most old houses had native timber on the floors.

"They come up beautifully with modern finishes," he added.

"Glen's a frustrated handyman," Maddie told her. "He wanted us to buy an old villa and fix it up, but living in the middle of renovations would drive me crazy. We have friends who've been 'doing up' for years!"

"This will be a big job for one woman," Glen commented. "You're not planning to do everything yourself are you, Paige?"

"It's already been rewired and reroofed. I'll hire professionals to fix cupboards in the kitchen and renovate the bathroom. But I hope to do a lot."

"I'm a dab hand with a paintbrush," Glen said.

Maddie rolled her eyes. "For heaven's sake, Paige, take pity on the poor guy and let him help you."

Laughing, Paige said, "I'll take all the help I can get." Glen's attitude was refreshing after her father's frowning comment that she should have asked his advice before being talked into a lemon by a slick real estate agent, and her mother's scarcely concealed horror.

"There!" Maddie kissed Glen lightly. "You're hired."

He grinned down at her, hooking an arm around her waist to kiss her back. Paige looked on with a pang of envy. She was glad Maddie had found someone who obviously adored her and was committed to sharing their future. But in comparison her own future looked bleak and lonely.

"By the way," Maddie said, breaking reluctantly away, "we're having a dinner party Saturday night for the families, mine and Glen's. You're invited, of course."

Of course she was, and of course she had to go. It wasn't until the day before the party that Maddie told her Jager would be there too. "Glen took it for granted that his family includes Jager now. His mother is being awfully good since she found out. She told Jager he's welcome in their home anytime. You will still come, won't you? Only I thought I should warn you, when I realized what Glen had done."

"Are you going to warn Mother and Dad too?"

Maddie groaned. "I suppose I should. I hope this party isn't going to be a disaster!"

"It won't. Mother will turn on her best manners, and Dad will follow her lead."

And as for her, Paige resolved, she would do her utmost to ensure that Maddie's first postwedding party went as smoothly as possible.

When Paige arrived at Maddie and Glen's third-floor apartment in the central city, Jager was already there, looking relaxed and urbane with a shot glass in his hand and talking to Glen's parents.

Maddie ushered Paige in and Jager got up, crossing the thick deep blue carpet to kiss her cheek. "Paige," he said, "how are you?"

Even that light touch sent a tingle right to her toes. Without quite meeting his eyes, she said she was fine, thank you, and how was his injured leg?

"No problems. I told you it was only bruised."

Glen asked her what she'd like to drink, and somehow she found herself seated next to Jager on one of the three leather couches arranged in a U shape. The room was a picture of understated modern elegance. Glen was a junior partner in his father's law firm, and Maddie worked for an advertising company. Their family connections ensured they had no need to be upwardly mobile, nor, despite Glen's yen to be a handyman, any need to do their own decorating.

Glen's mother said, "You two know each other?"

While Paige was wondering how much her sister had told Glen, Jager said, "We knew each other very well at one time." He glanced at Paige. "It's not exactly a secret. As a matter of fact, we were married."

Mrs. Provost's mouth opened in surprise. "Married?"

Paige said, "It was a long time ago. We were very young and...it didn't last long."

Mr. Provost raised his eyebrows and shook his head. "New Zealand is such a small country, but...well. Quite a coincidence."

Glen handed Paige a glass that she accepted gratefully, glad to have something to concentrate on. His mother said, "Did you know this, Glen?"

He cast an apologetic look at Paige. "Maddie told me."

Paige took a gulp of the wine he'd given her. "As Jager says, it's no secret."

"I'm glad to see you can still be friends," Mrs. Provost said warmly. "I do think it's sad when two people who've found they made a mistake can hardly be civil to each other."

"So do I," Jager agreed.

Friendship had never entered into the equation, Paige thought, looking back. Their feelings had been too raw and white-hot for anything so tepid as that. And their marriage had ended in recrimination and bitterness. They'd been hurting too much to entertain any possibility of remaining friends.

Her eyes met Jager's and she searched for some clue to his emotions. If he cared about his newfound brother as she certainly cared about her sister, they would have to come to some kind of accommodation. This wouldn't be the last time they'd find themselves involved in a family occasion.

As Paige had predicted, her parents accepted Jager's presence with a show of equanimity. After the meal her father was deep in conversation with him while her mother talked with Maddie and Mrs. Provost.

Glen was picking up emptied coffee cups and offering refills, and Paige went to help. "Thanks, Paige," he said as she followed him to the kitchen, where the counter was filled with dinner dishes and cooking utensils roughly piled together. "We'll stack the dishwasher later." He balanced cups and saucers precariously on top of one of the piles.

"I'll stack it," Paige offered. "You go back to your guests."

She had made some headway and was bending over the machine to slot a plate into one of the last spaces left when she heard someone come in.

Straightening, she said, "Nearly there," and turned, expecting to see Glen or Maddie.

Jager stood in the doorway, holding a couple of empty wine bottles and some used glasses. "Maddie wondered where you'd got to," he told her. "Lawrence and Paula are leaving."

"You call your father by his first name?"

"It seems a bit late to be calling him Dad."

"I'm glad you found him," she said. "It must be…" She faltered, unable to imagine how it would be to find a father you had never known. "What about your mother?"

"She's dead."

"Oh, Jager…I'm sorry."

He shrugged. "Don't waste your sympathy. I never knew her."

"I always thought that was sad. For both of you."

"It was her choice. Are you going to come and say goodbye?"

She went ahead of him back to the living room.

Her parents had decided to leave too, and after a decent interval and another cup of coffee Paige said she must be going.

Jager echoed her, and they rode down together to the ground floor. When the elevator doors swished apart he followed her into the lobby and opened the outer door for her.

"I'll walk you to your car," he said.

He accompanied her in silence, but as she unlocked the door of her new little hatchback he said, "We need to talk, Paige."

With the key in her hand, she straightened. "We talked tonight."

The conversation had flowed remarkably easily

considering the possible tensions in the room. Jager had easily discussed the news of the day, business and politics with incisive, well-thought-out opinions, and made the others laugh a couple of times with his understated but razorlike humor.

Even her mother's perfect but lukewarm courtesy warmed and shifted to reluctant graciousness when he'd shown an appreciation of one of her favorite composers. And Paige had enjoyed lightly sparring with him over their differing views of a recent hit film.

He said impatiently, "You know what I meant— we need to talk about...this."

His hand was under her chin, and he crowded her against the car as he turned her and brought his lips down on hers, compelling and insistent.

She managed to resist the temptation to kiss him back, not fighting him but staying rigid in his arms.

He lifted his head but didn't move away.

Her voice husky, Paige said, "That isn't talking, either."

Jager gave a short, breathy laugh. His hands left her and he placed them on the roof of the car, trapping her in the circle of his arms. "It's a start."

"No," she said, suddenly angry. "It isn't a start of anything. It's a leftover—from something that finished long ago."

"Finished?"

"Finished. Finito. Over. Dead."

"And what about the night of your sister's wedding? Was that a leftover? It didn't feel dead to me."

"That was an aberration, a stupid impulse that

should never have happened. *Would* never have happened if it hadn't been for the accident.''

''Okay, if you need an excuse, go ahead. It doesn't change anything. That night you wanted me as much as I wanted you, for whatever reason you care to cook up.''

''You don't understand!''

''The hell I don't! You can't stand the thought that you slept with me six months after your husband died, so you need something to blame it on—you weren't yourself, you were in shock, you didn't know what you were doing. But don't try to make me swallow your theories, honey. We both wanted it, we both enjoyed it.'' His hard voice dropped to a seductive murmur. ''And I promise you'll enjoy it next time…and the next, and the next. Once you can bring yourself to admit that you still want me.''

Paige was trembling. He couldn't have made it more clear that he had no interest in her as anything other than a sex object, and that he was convinced she felt the same about him. ''You arrogant…sod!'' Even in anger she couldn't bring herself to call him a bastard, knowing what she did about his parentage. ''Try this for an excuse, then! My husband was *killed* in a car crash!''

CHAPTER FOUR

JAGER glared at her for several seconds, assimilating that. His throat moved before he said hoarsely, "I didn't know."

"Well now you do," she said. "So maybe you can begin to see why I was so shaken up that night. Why I would have done anything to help me forget..."

"With anyone?" he queried harshly.

Chewing on her lip, she looked away.

At last he moved, dropping his hands and taking a step back.

Paige looked down at the key in her hand. She turned to open the door, and Jager leaned forward and did it for her.

"I'll see you again," he said, making her pause.

"I suppose so."

"Count on it."

About to climb into the car, she turned her head to him. "Jager—for Maddie's sake, and Glen's, can't we be friends?"

"Can't friends be lovers?"

That was how it had been with her and Aidan. Friends, then lovers, then husband and wife. But not with Jager. "Friends can become lovers," she conceded, "but—"

"I suppose it's too much to hope that's a promise."

"It isn't a promise! I wasn't talking about us."

"I thought that was exactly what we were doing."

He wouldn't give up easily. He'd always been tenacious and clever. Presumably that had got him where he was today, a successful, dynamic young businessman, with few signs of the rough edges that had so grated on her parents when he was younger, and made them anxious for their daughter's welfare.

Closing her eyes, she said, "I'm tired, Jager. I don't want to fight."

"No one's fighting," he said. "Except maybe you. Does it count that you're fighting yourself?" His hand touched her arm. "Good night, Paige."

She didn't answer, getting into the driver's seat and settling herself without looking at him again, even when he closed the door and let her drive away.

Glen had promised to be at the cottage the following weekend, when Paige intended to start painting the exterior, but she was surprised to see Maddie hop out of the car too.

When the rear door opened and Jager uncoiled his long legs and stood up, she felt her heart lurch and her welcoming smile falter.

Maddie's eyes were anxious as she approached her sister, with a cloth-covered basket in her hands. "I made some muffins for the workers. Jager called in when we were leaving, and Glen brought him along to help. Do you mind?"

Glen said, "You told us you'd use all the help you could get."

Jager was looking at the cottage, his gaze going from the new roof to the shabby walls. As Maddie finished her breathless speech he brought his eyes to Paige and lifted his brows in silent inquiry.

"I don't mind," she said mechanically. Annoyingly, she was conscious of the shabbiness of her stained jeans and faded, baggy T-shirt. Maddie, in stretch-fit pants and scoop-necked blue silk-knit top, with a matching blue ribbon in her hair, looked fresh and sparkling and quite delicious. And Jager's beige slacks and white open-necked shirt didn't remotely resemble work clothes.

Glen, dressed for action in old shorts and a disreputable T-shirt, rummaged in the back of the car and tossed a gray bundle to his half brother. "Here, Jay."

The bundle unraveled into a pair of workmanlike overalls as Jager caught it. Maddie was moving toward the kitchen, Glen inspecting the walls, and Jager paused in front of Paige. "If you want me to leave," he said quietly, "say the word. I'll square it with Glen."

"There's no need." She couldn't avoid him forever without making things awkward for her sister. "It's good of you to help."

His gaze returned briefly to the cottage. "You've taken on quite a task here."

"It keeps me occupied, which is what I need." Sanding back paint and filling holes and gaps was therapy. The physical work sent her to bed ready to sleep, instead of tossing restlessly as she had in her parents' house.

She saw curiosity in his eyes followed by comprehension, and then a strangely wooden expression settled on his face.

Glen turned to them and called, "Right, where shall we start?"

Jager and Glen painted the exterior walls, and Maddie helped Paige color the window frames. The morning went quickly, and the sun made the paint dry fast and brought the men out in a sweat.

Glen ripped off his shirt and wiped his forehead with it. "I could do with a swim."

Unzipping the overalls, Jager said, "The sea's right at the bottom of Paige's garden."

Glen grinned. "Yeah."

"You don't have swimming togs," Maddie objected.

"Who needs them?" Glen looked at Jager, who dropped the overalls to reveal a pair of snug black briefs. Paige hadn't realized he wasn't wearing his clothes.

Glen said, "What's it like down there, Paige?"

"There's a little shingly beach and some flat rocks. The water's deep enough to swim quite close to the shore, and it's usually calm."

Glen looked at Jager, who nodded. Paige said, "I'll get you some towels."

"You're not coming?" Jager queried when she handed him one.

She shook her head. "Maddie and I will have lunch ready when you come back."

The men came back with their wet underwear plastered to them and the towels slung around their necks. Maddie made a show of being impressed by Glen's state of undress, running a hand over his bare chest and cooing at him. Jager, the black briefs clinging to his hips, gave Paige a blatant come-on look which she ignored, although she couldn't help a smile twitching the corner of her mouth before she turned away.

When the men had dressed the four of them sat on the little porch eating sandwiches and the scones, Maddie and Glen shoulder to shoulder on the bottom step, Paige and Jager facing each other with their backs against the corner posts at the top, their legs carefully not touching.

A neighbor walking his dog waved at them as he passed. Paige waved back. She felt happier than she had for ages.

Jager shoved back a lock of damp hair and swallowed a bite of his sandwich. "D'you know him?"

"He lives just down the street."

"Alone?"

"I don't know. He walks the dog every day and we say hello. People are friendly round here."

"How many of them know you're living alone?"

She stared at him. "No idea. I haven't broadcast the fact."

"You'll need a burglar alarm. Have you done anything about that?"

"I'm not sure I want one." She almost laughed. "Dad said that too." It was so rarely the two of them agreed on anything.

"He was right."

Paige wet a thumb and raised it. "Chalk that up."

"It's no joke," Jager said. "I know a good firm. I'll get them to send someone round to give you a quote."

"I can get my own quotes, thanks."

"*Paige*—" He seemed about to say something sharp, but pulled himself up. Moderating his tone to mildness, he said, "Let me do this. It's only a quote. No obligation."

Paige inspected the filling in her sandwich, giving herself time. No harm, she supposed, in agreeing. "All right." She shrugged. "Thanks for the offer."

They worked until dark and then stopped for a meal that the two women scraped together from what was in the kitchen, and sat for a while in lazy companionship, sipping coffee. Jager hadn't talked very much but the other two made up for that. Paige was conscious of his gaze brushing her, producing a physical reaction, a light feathering across her skin, but they'd hardly spoken to each other all day.

Glen suggested another swim. "And why don't you girls come too?"

Maddie shook her head. "Paige said it's deep, and in the dark...? No thanks."

"Got a torch, Paige?" Glen asked.

She rummaged in the kitchen drawers and handed it to him.

"What about you?" he asked her, and when she shook her head he said, "Still afraid of deep waters, Paige?"

It would be silly and childish to rise to such a blatant dare. "I'm not in the mood."

After they'd gone Maddie said, "Do you really think you can make something of this place?"

"You wait." Paige started picking up coffee cups. "It'll be as good as new. Better. Thanks for letting

Glen help.'' She pecked Maddie's cheek in passing. ''He's been great. You too. I didn't expect you to turn up.''

''And Jager.''

''And Jager,'' Paige agreed.

Maddie followed her into the half-renovated kitchen. ''Isn't it funny the way things turn out? I mean, me being sort of related to Jager.''

''It's a small world.''

''I suppose Aidan *was* more your type, really. Mum and Dad's type, anyway...''

''My type too,'' Paige said firmly, starting to rinse cups. ''Aidan and I understood each other. I was lucky to find him.''

''He was one of the nicest men I've ever met,'' Maddie said warmly, finding a tea towel. ''A lot like Glen.''

Paige gave her sister an affectionate smile. ''Yes.''

''Not that I don't like Jager. But he's...different. Harder. I was a bit worried when I found out he's Glen's half brother.''

''About me?''

''About Glen.'' Maddie looked at her apologetically. ''You too, of course. But Glen was so pleased to have found a brother, keen to get close, make Jager feel like one of the family, and Jager...well, he was kind of aloof at first, as if he was weighing us all up. I wasn't sure if he really liked any of us—even Glen or his father. I wondered if he had some kind of hidden agenda, but maybe he just needed time to get used to the idea that he had a family.''

"Jager's never been really close to anyone," Paige said. She knew exactly what Maddie meant.

"Not even you, when you were married?" Maddie's eyes widened.

"I thought he was but...some people are not good at relationships."

"With his background, not surprising. Is that why you broke up?"

"It wasn't all his fault," Paige said hastily. "We were both too young for that kind of commitment. And too different."

Maddie nodded. "Is it okay for him to come again tomorrow? If you don't want him just say. I'll talk to Glen. I was a bit wild that he brought him along without asking you, but—" a frown creased the perfect skin between her fine brows "—I guess it seemed a good idea to him."

"Sure it's okay." Glen was doing her a favor and if he wanted Jager along, it shouldn't hurt her to accommodate his wishes.

They finished the dishes and Paige showed Maddie what she intended to do with the interior of the house.

"Well, better you than me, but I expect you'll work wonders," Maddie said. "That's one thing you inherited from Mum, an eye for design and color. I'm hopeless with anything like that. Wouldn't know where to start. Clothes, now...that's different!" She yawned. "The men are taking a long time. There's a torch in the car. Why don't we go down and hurry them up."

The path was short but rough. Paige went ahead with the torch, emerging at the bottom from the manuka and tree ferns onto crushed shells and tiny pebbles mixed with soft dark sand. The water lapped in low ripples along the narrow shoreline, and across the harbor Auckland was a glowing blur of city lights with the illuminated Sky Tower rising above the others. A pale half-moon cast a sheen on the glassy blackness of the sea.

The men were still in the water, making muted silver splashes. Maddie called to them, and after a quick sweep of the torch, picking up their glistening faces and arms, Paige switched off the light.

Glen said, "Come in, Mad. It's great."

Maddie laughed. "You're nuts. Both of you. Anyway, I don't have anything to put on."

Glen said patiently, "It's dark, love. No need to put on anything. We didn't."

"You're skinny-dipping?"

"Why not? We're the only ones here."

"It's cold—"

"Not that cold, and once you're in it warms up. Live a little dangerously. I'll look after you, promise."

After a few more seconds of hesitation Maddie pulled the pale knitted top over her head and said nervously to Paige, "Do you think I could swim in my undies?"

"Everything will cling when you come out with them wet," Paige warned. "If you're worried about your modesty you'd be better off nude."

"Oh. I suppose you're right."

A louder splash carried to shore, and Paige

glimpsed the line of an arm raised in a crawl. Jager, she guessed, because Glen was still trying to coax his wife into the water.

"I'm coming," Maddie called bravely, and waded in, squealing before she plunged in and swam to Glen's side.

They exchanged some laughing murmurs, and Paige sat on the cool sand and waited.

She couldn't see Jager anymore. Or hear him, she realized. Her eyes hunted the dark water. "Where's Jager?" she called sharply.

"Over there," Glen called back, but she couldn't see him clearly enough to know where he meant. "I think."

He *thought?* How long was it since she'd seen that arm, apparently heading out into the harbor?

She switched on the torch again, to sweep the beam over the sea. It found Maddie and Glen, their arms around each other, and Maddie squealed again in laughing protest.

"Sorry." Paige stood up and moved the beam across the inky surface. Where was he? She crunched forward over the shingle until the cold water seeping into her canvas shoes brought her up with a small shock.

Instinctively she retreated a step, then put down the torch and began tearing off her clothes. Blind panic fluttered in her throat.

She was down to her bra and briefs when Jager's voice nearby said, "Decided to join us?"

Paige jumped, and swallowed a scream. "Where were you?" she said, swinging toward the voice, seeing a large glistening shape against paler rocks at the water's edge. "Have you been there all the time?"

"All what time? I was in the water until half a minute ago. You're going in?"

He didn't know she'd been looking for him. That she'd had some mad idea of diving in and rescuing him. Maybe he'd been underwater when she'd missed him. She remembered he'd always been able to hold his breath for long periods beneath the surface. "Yes," she said, trying to sound nonchalant. "Just a short dip."

Paige could scarcely make him out in the darkness. So it followed he couldn't see her, either. Quickly she dispensed with her bra and panties and waded in, getting under the water as soon as she could.

She breast-stroked parallel to the shore, a little further out than the other two, who were playing around like a couple of dolphins—or a couple in love. As Paige and Jager had once done, chasing and splashing each other, then falling silent as they glided near, touched, even kissed until the water closed over their heads and they had to surface...

Paige turned on her back and looked up at the pale stars that competed with the city lights. She'd been floating for a few minutes when Jager's voice close by interrupted her reverie. "Paige?"

"What?" She turned over, treading water.

"Just checking you're okay. I couldn't see you."

Paige almost laughed. Him too? "I'm getting out."

She started back to the shore, and found him beside her, matching stroke for stroke.

They splashed to the shingly sand together, and Jager said, ''Where's the torch?''

She didn't remember exactly. ''Over here, I think.'' Heading off blindly, she stumbled over a smooth rock embedded in the sand, and found herself on her knees.

Jager dropped beside her. ''Are you all right?'' One of his hands brushed her water-slicked breast. ''Sorry,'' he muttered, as she drew in a startled breath. His hand found her arm and closed on wet, slippery skin.

Paige could scarcely breathe. She was suddenly hotly conscious of her nakedness—and his. And of the delicious tingling where he'd touched her. She pulled away, repudiating her feelings. ''I'm not hurt,'' she said. ''I need my clothes.''

''Stay there, I'll find them.''

He left her and found the torch, hunted down her crumpled clothes and turned off the light before giving them to her along with a towel.

''Thanks.'' She dried off, scrambled into her clothes, and was thankful when the other two came out of the water, arms still around each other, and with much muffled laughter got dressed.

On the way back Maddie and Glen took one of the lights and led the way, walking hand in hand. He turned his head to kiss the top of hers.

Paige shone the other torch on the path for herself and Jager. A trickle of water ran coldly down her neck to the neckline of her T-shirt. Her hair still hung in wet rat's tails. Maddie had tied hers into a topknot before going into the water and somehow kept it almost totally dry.

Paige sighed, and Jager said, "Something the matter?"

"I'm a bit tired." Her T-shirt was clammy because her hasty drying had been less than thorough. She was conscious of Jager beside her. They weren't even touching, yet she was sure she could feel the warmth emanating from him, and smell the scent of his skin mingled with the salty tang of seawater. To take her mind off it she said, "You and Glen have done wonders. It was rather a cheek for him to rope you in."

For an instant she saw his smile flash, a glimpse of white teeth. "Thanks for not sending me away."

He had surprised her with his offer to go. "Would you have gone?" Perhaps he'd counted on her unwillingness to upset her sister. Maybe it had been a bluff.

"Whatever you wanted," he said smoothly. Which told her nothing. "I'd like to come back tomorrow."

Paige shrugged, trying to convey supreme indifference. "A tiger for punishment," she said lightly. "Please yourself."

After they'd gone she had a quick shower and went to bed in the spare room. When she closed her eyes she could see against the darkness the outline of Jager's masculine form, naked as he had been on the little beach, more clearly than she had in reality. She felt again the brush of his hand against her, and her body yearned for him.

She turned on her back and opened her eyes, trying to dispel the tormenting images. Deliberately she conjured up a mental picture of Aidan. Gentle Aidan, who had been sweet and funny and had helped mend her wounded heart, who had taught her that the wound wasn't mortal after all. Aidan, who deserved at least a proper period of mourning.

But thinking about him only made her sad, and when her lids drifted down again and she slipped into sleep, it was to dream erotically of Jager.

By Sunday evening the cottage walls gleamed a warm pinkish cream, the trims a dark dusky rose.

Jager's promised contact visited Paige on Monday with brochures and advice on security, leaving her with a couple of quotes. Afterward Jager phoned to check the man had been and said, "You won't mess around on this, will you? You need something in place as soon as possible."

"It's a quiet neighborhood," she protested.

"Women have been attacked in quiet neighborhoods," Jager said. "Get it done, Paige."

"You're not my keeper!"

"I want to be sure you're safe."

She was an independent woman, Paige reminded herself, who could fend quite well for herself. Yet his concern lit a warm glow in her heart, as if he'd put strong, protective arms around her. And it was decidedly galling to realize that she liked it.

CHAPTER FIVE

As THE renovations progressed it seemed tacitly taken for granted that Jager as well as Glen was involved in the makeover. Paige almost became used to his presence alongside his half brother.

They helped lift the old carpets and the layers of even older cracked lino that a preliminary investigation had shown underneath. Taking a short break, Glen ran a hand through his thick brown hair, rubbed at it and grimaced. "I could do with a shower."

Paige knew how he felt. The dust and grime of years had worked its way through the carpet fibers. Even Jager was grime-streaked, his hair dusty. She probably looked as though she needed a shower too.

"Feel free to use the bathroom," she said, sitting back to rub black dust from her glasses on a corner of her shirt. "Although it isn't very glamorous at the moment." They'd ripped up the flooring in there too, and everything was covered in fine, gritty debris. "Or you could swim."

Bending back to the job in hand, Glen said, "A swim would take too long. Let's finish this sucker."

Jager looked over at Paige. "Why don't you go and clean up, and leave the rest to us?"

She shook her head. This was her project and although grateful for the help she wouldn't sit back and let them do it for her.

Maddie was as fresh as ever. She'd been wonderful at providing sustenance for the others and fetching and carrying, but drew the line at going down on her hands and knees and getting physical. When the old carpets and pieces of flooring had been shoved into the hired bin at the gate, she told Paige, "You'd better sleep over at our place. Your bed's under all that furniture the men shifted."

They'd moved everything movable into one room to clear the other floors.

"There wasn't much." Jager looked at her questioningly. "You don't seem to have a lot."

"I didn't want the place cluttered up with furniture while I was renovating."

It would have been sensible, Paige supposed, to have the floors finished before she moved in, but once the cottage was hers she'd been impatient to start living in it, making plans for its restoration.

"You must have had furniture and things in America," Jager observed.

"There didn't seem much point in transporting it all that way." It had been hard but she'd sold or given away almost everything she and Aidan had owned, keeping only a few pictures and some knickknacks for their sentimental value.

"You just left it?" He paused. "Yes, I suppose you would. Cutting your losses."

Even Glen looked a bit disconcerted. Maddie glanced from Jager to Paige. "You must be exhausted," she said to her sister. "Let's get you over to our place and find you a bed."

Sliding between cool sheets an hour later, Paige

consciously tried to relax. Despite the men's help with the physical labor her muscles ached. And something else ached—something in the region of her heart.

Her dreams were filled with images of Jager—Jager accusing and angry, his green eyes hard as glass, saying something she couldn't hear. Jager wielding a paint brush, laughing. And then Jager walking toward her, taking her in his arms, bearing her down on a shingly midnight beach that in the way of dreams became a soft, rocking bed, a black satin sea on which they miraculously floated as they made passionate, sweet love until they sank into the water and a dark oblivion.

The morning was still new when Maddie came into her room. "Did you sleep well?"

"I slept okay," Paige said. Her sister looked blooming. She hadn't had to rely on dreams.

Maddie seemed to want to say something more, and finally decided to take the plunge. "It's a bit soon to be bringing it up, but you're young to be a widow, Paige. And it would be nice if…"

"I'm sure it would, from your point of view," Paige said crisply. And Glen's, maybe. A nice neat equation. "It won't work, though. Didn't before and can't now."

Maddie pouted but didn't press the point.

Paige brushed away the remnants of her dreams, banishing them to the ether. "I'd better get up."

When Paige had patiently removed stubborn rusted carpet tacks and ensured there were no protruding nails or splintered boards, she hired a professional to sand the floors, which turned out to be kauri as Glen had predicted.

During the long Easter break he and Jager helped apply polyurethane to protect and bring out the grain of the wood, and while each coat dried they all tackled the overgrown shrubs and vines in the neglected garden. Even Maddie donned gardening gloves to pull weeds and reveal long-forgotten plant treasures, while the men chainsawed a tree whose rotting trunk endangered the new roof.

Paige stayed at Maddie and Glen's apartment to escape the fumes while the floors dried.

"That's that," Glen said, as he cleaned the last of the brushes. "Another twenty-four hours and then we can move the furniture from the bedroom and do that floor."

"I can manage that one room on my own," Paige said. "I owe you all. Dinner's on me. Where shall we go?"

"I'm not fit to go anywhere!" Maddie objected, although there was hardly a spot on her pink cotton top and stretch jeans.

Glen flexed his shoulders and yawned. "Why don't we just head back to our place and see what we can scratch up?"

In the end they decided on pizzas that Paige insisted she would pay for. And this time, back at the apartment, Jager joined them.

Glen poured wine to go with the pizzas, and they ate in the kitchen, crowding around the small table. Maddie and Glen were in high spirits, Glen plying Paige with far more wine than she was accustomed to. She felt relaxed and warm and well-fed, and the happy glow that surrounded her sister and brother-in-law affected her too.

Jager lounged in a chair, one thumb tucked into the waistband of his jeans, a faint smile on his mouth and lazy lids concealing his eyes. He seemed to be watching his half brother with almost clinical fascination, and for a moment Paige felt as if a cold draught had entered the room. He switched his gaze to Maddie, who was getting giggly.

Maddie's eyes were bright, her cheeks flushed like a rose. She smiled a trifle muzzily when she found Jager looking at her. That smile would have melted stone, and Paige was relieved to see him smile back, his expression softening.

Glen leaned across and poured more wine into Jager's glass, emptying the bottle. "I'll fetch another one," he announced.

"Not for me," Jager protested. "I have to drive home."

"Get a taxi or stay here," Glen said. "Plenty of couches to choose from." He opened a fresh bottle and Jager didn't protest at his glass being filled to the top.

Things became hazy after that. At some stage they shifted to the living room, more wine appeared and Glen put on some music. He and Maddie danced a little, their arms wrapped around each other, and then Maddie yawned and announced she was going to bed.

She walked uncertainly toward the door, tripped on something invisible and said, "Oops!"

Glen swooped to steady her. "Come on, love," he

said. "One foot after the other." Looking back, he said, "You two will be okay if I don't come back?"

Sitting opposite Paige, one arm resting on the back of a couch, Jager raised his glass. "Sure. Good night."

Paige was nursing half a glass of wine. She put it down on a side table, and got up to turn off the music.

Into the resultant silence Jager said, "Spoilsport."

She turned to him. "Did you want it on?"

"Only if you're going to dance with me." His eyes sent her a brazen invitation.

Paige shook her head. The room swayed, and she said, "I doubt if I'm capable. What do you suppose is in that wine?"

"I think we're probably suffering from the effects of fumes from stuff we put on the floor, combined with alcohol."

"You too?" She eyed him doubtfully. He looked the same as always—unruffled, handsome, contained.

"Put it this way—I'm not driving home." He downed the rest of the liquid in his glass. "I don't suppose you'd like to share the spare bed with me?"

"I'm slightly under the weather," she said, "but not that much."

Jager laughed. "I guess I'd better call a cab."

He didn't move, and neither did she. They were almost at opposite ends of the room, and yet Paige felt as if a golden cobweb was being spun about them, binding them.

She shook herself, a physical movement to bring her back to reality.

"What was that for?" Jager got up from the couch and came toward her, his feet soundless on the carpet.

"Keeping myself awake," she said. "It's been a tiring few days."

"Don't work yourself too hard. I'll help Glen shift things out of the bedroom tomorrow night."

"You've been awfully helpful. Thank you."

"I wanted to do it."

"Why?"

"You think I have an ulterior motive?"

"Don't you always?"

He laughed. "Below the belt, Paige. And untrue."

"Is it?" she asked wistfully. "I don't know."

He frowned at her. "Have you the faintest idea what you're talking about? Because I don't."

"Maybe not, maybe it's the wine." She had just begun to grasp at a thought but it eluded her. Somehow it seemed important and yet she couldn't put it into words. "Did you ever really love me?"

His eyes darkened, and his face became a mask. The words hung in the air between them. She despised herself for uttering them. But the question had been lurking in her subconscious for years. Right back to the very first time he'd told her he loved her, and she'd wanted so much to believe it that she'd pushed aside her instinctive doubt and decided to ride the dream.

"What do you think?" he said, turning the question back at her. "My God, if you have to ask me..."

"*Did you?*" she said. "Or did you think you were marrying my father's money?" It was too late to retract, and suddenly she desperately needed an answer.

He looked as though he would rather kill her. She blinked at the ferocity in his stare, in his voice when at last he spoke, the tone shockingly at odds with the words.

"I thought the world revolved around you," he said. "That the moon and stars would disappear into black, endless night if you left me. When that happened, I thought I'd die. The sun would never shine again and nothing in the wide world could ever make things right. You were the center of my soul and the thing that kept my heart beating, you gave me a reason for taking every breath. Does that sound like love?"

Paige was dizzy. She couldn't speak. Her lips parted, but while she was trying to fumble words to her tongue he laughed, making her cringe. "I was wrong, of course," he said almost conversationally. "The world didn't stop and I went on breathing, and eating and walking around. Everything continued just as before, until one day I realized how little it had all mattered, really."

How little *she* had mattered? Paige swallowed a lump of unreasonable hurt.

He went on, "One more broken heart doesn't stop the world. One woman had let me down—but there were plenty of other women around, once I stopped nursing my wounds and feeling sorry for myself."

"You didn't marry any of them!" she blurted, stung by a shaft of unwarranted jealousy.

"Like I said, I don't make the same mistake twice."

"Neither do I."

He was silent for a moment. "So you don't want another wedding ring from me?"

Immediately she repudiated that. "Good God, no! Didn't we make enough of a mess of it the first time?"

His laughter this time signaled genuine amusement. "At least we agree on that." He gave her a long, considering look. "But the sex was great. It still is…judging by the night of Maddie's wedding."

Paige wasn't sure what was causing the hollowed feeling in her midriff. Any relationship involving sex was out of the question. She tilted her head in defiance. "I don't want a wedding ring," she said, "and I won't sleep with you, either."

"Impasse," he drawled, looking as though he couldn't take it seriously.

Uneasy, she tried to hide it, refusing to look away from the glinting green eyes. "Are you going to call that cab?"

He didn't move immediately, but then with a faint shrug he crossed to the telephone on the wall and dialed. "Don't let me keep you up," he said as he turned after hanging up. "I'll wait for it outside."

Paige nodded. "Good night, then."

"Good night." He started to make for the door, then swerved and fetched up in front of her again. Not touching her with his hands, he bent and brushed a kiss against her mouth. "Sweet dreams."

She stood rock-still, her hands unconsciously clenched at her sides as he let himself out.

The following evening the men moved the furniture and laid the first coat of polish on the bedroom floor.

Maddie and Glen left but Jager lingered by the open door. He said, "What's the next step, Paige?"

She chose to take him literally. "Stripping the walls ready for hanging new papers, painting skirtings."

"Need help with that?"

"Not really. I'm in no hurry and it gives me something to do."

He frowned at her. "Why so desperate?"

"Desperate?"

"To fill every waking moment." He reached out and took one of her hands, ignoring her surprised resistance. Turning it in his, he studied her palm. It was roughened from working on the garden and in the house, and she had tiny blisters on the pads below her fingers. "Why are you doing this to yourself?" he asked.

Paige pulled away. "I'm enjoying finding what's hidden away under those layers of paint and paper. Once all that's stripped off this place will be beautiful, the way it was when it was first lived in by people who loved and cared for it."

"Loved it? How do you know that?"

"Laugh if you like, but I sense it was a home where people were secure and happy."

"I'm not laughing." He was looking at her curiously. "Were you secure and happy—before your husband died?"

Paige blinked at him, disconcerted at the change of subject. "Yes. Very happy."

He searched her face as if he wanted to catch her out in a lie. But it wasn't a lie, and she stared fearlessly back at him. Finally he gave a curt nod. "I'm glad."

He looked around them. "Do you think a house can give that back to you?"

"I think it's what I need right now."

"But not all you need."

She agreed cautiously. "I need my family too. My job. Friends."

"Is that enough?"

"For now."

"It isn't much." He sounded almost contemptuous.

"It's a lot. Plenty of people don't have those things."

"True." A corner of his mouth turned down.

Paige bit her lip. He wasn't reminding her, but when they'd met he'd been unemployed, friendless in a strange city, and had no one. She said, "I don't mean to reopen old wounds."

He smiled tightly. "They don't hurt anymore."

"You found your family—your father."

"He found me. I wasn't looking."

That was a surprise. "I thought you must have…"

"Changed my mind?" He shook his head. "I don't need him."

That's what he'd said when he'd told her that his father was some spoiled rich kid who had got a teen-age girl pregnant and then scarpered. His name didn't even appear on Jager's birth certificate. Now he added, with the same note of indifference verging on contempt, "If he's discovered some need to salve his conscience after all this time, it's no skin off my nose."

"Don't you feel anything for him?"

Hands in his pockets, he regarded her. "Should I?"

"He's your father, and I know it's late in the day, but if he went to the trouble of finding you, he must have some sense of...responsibility."

Jager laughed. "I'm responsible for myself. Always have been. That's not going to change."

"How did he find you?" Paige moved to the couch and sat down.

After a moment Jager followed, sitting half facing her on the other end, one arm draped along the back. "He hired a detective. The guy found the aunt up north who cared for me after my mother walked out on me."

Paige recalled the insouciance hiding an underlying bitterness with which he'd first told her that when he was only a few months old his mother dumped him with an aunt who had several children of her own, while she traveled from the small country town of his birth to the city. She'd send the aunt a little money now and then, but she never came back, never sent for him. And after a while the money stopped.

When he was five the aunt had packed his belongings into a bag and told him a nice lady was coming to take him to a new mum and dad. He hadn't understood what it meant. "I guess she'd had enough," he said when Paige asked why. "She hadn't asked to be saddled with an extra kid, she had enough on her hands with her own family, and I was probably a brat even then."

He'd been hardly more than a baby, Paige had thought indignantly. The first foster home lasted until the couple started a family of their own. When the new baby arrived they asked the department to take Jager away.

"That was mean!" she'd exclaimed when he told her.

"They never promised to keep me forever." He shrugged. "It wasn't their fault I was too young to understand the concept of temporary foster care."

She'd sensed his hurt at the third rejection in his then short life. No wonder his next foster parents had found him difficult to deal with and finally given up. As did several others.

By the time the department found a successful placement for him, he had lost the will for a real relationship with anyone, keeping his emotions guarded behind a wall of indifference.

Not that he'd ever said so. Paige had deduced a lot of what she knew about him from offhand, unguarded remarks rather than heart-to-heart confessional talks. Jager had never been big on verbal communication.

He'd been smart enough, she gathered, to see for himself eventually that making trouble didn't get him anywhere. And that no one could look after him as well as he could himself.

Following skirmishes with teachers and a couple of minor brushes with the law as a teenager, involving underage drinking, illegal drag races and a couple of street fights, he'd left school and found a temporary job on a fishing trawler.

A couple more jobs followed before he'd gone south.

"To find your mother?" Paige had asked him.

He laughed. "Why?" he demanded derisively. "She doesn't want me turning up on her doorstep. And I wouldn't cross the street to give her the time of day."

Work in the city wasn't easy to find, and when he walked into a charity shop looking for secondhand clothing to replenish his meager wardrobe he'd had no job and no prospects.

Paige, in school uniform and with her shoulder-length hair in two neat pigtails, was serving behind the counter as she did twice a week. Her school catered to Auckland's elite who could afford to pay its substantial fees, but the staff tried to instil a social conscience into their pupils. When an appeal was made for the girls to consider helping out at the nearby shop after school, she put up her hand.

Most of the volunteers were elderly, but the clientele varied from university students buying funky retro outfits to young parents saving on clothing that their children would grow out of within months, and older people obviously down on their luck.

Paige's mother had wrinkled her nose at the idea. "Ugh! Dealing with other people's used clothes and discarded pots and pans—you don't know where they've been!"

"They're cleaned before they go on sale," Paige assured her.

"Still..." Margaret shuddered delicately, but hadn't vetoed the idea. She herself was involved in a couple of charities, although her activities were confined to committee work and fund-raising.

Paige was fascinated by the people she met at the

shop. And never more so than by the lean, darkly handsome young man who walked in one day and made for the racks of men's clothing.

Earlier she'd noticed him peering into the window with an air of indecision, but when her glance collided with his he'd moved away.

She'd glimpsed black, slightly unkempt hair falling across a tanned forehead, a flash of startling green eyes under brooding black brows, making her blink behind her round, steel-rimmed glasses. His hands had been thrust into the front pockets of disreputable tight jeans.

Then she'd forgotten about him while she packed secondhand crockery, embroidered sheets, cooking utensils into a box for an excited young couple setting up house. "See ya," the man said, hefting the box into his arms.

The girl, her face aglow, added, "We need *lots* more stuff for our place! We'll be back."

Paige smiled after them. One day she might be like them, in love and looking forward to a future with someone special, like the people in the secondhand romance novels that were among the most popular items in the shop, and which she sometimes took home to read.

An older staff member asked her to retrieve a large vase from the top shelf. Perched on a stepladder to hand the item down to the well-dressed, bargain-hunting matron who coveted it, Paige saw the young man again, just inside the doorway.

As she climbed down he cast a comprehensive gaze

around the cramped shop before strolling toward the menswear section.

After steering a young family to a basket of swimwear, Paige deftly rescued a pile of odd saucers from the toddler's inquisitive fingers, and presented him with a box of colored wooden cubes to keep him occupied while she helped an elderly customer compare price tags.

Back behind the counter, she saw the dark-haired young man looking through the clothing section.

Covertly she watched him push aside several hangers, pull a couple of shirts from the rail, put one back and go to the suits and trousers.

Paige walked over to him. "Can I help?"

He gave her the full force of those green eyes, reminding her of a cornered big cat, wary and ready to pounce if threatened.

Apparently deciding she was no threat, he flashed her a killer smile, and later she wondered if she'd fallen in love with him right there and then. It was enough to make any woman go weak at the knees. And Paige, young and inexperienced at sixteen but a woman all the same, was no exception.

"D'you think these'll fit me?" he asked her, holding out front-pleated dark plum pants, and then glancing down at the shabby but clean jeans he was wearing.

She looked down too, and blushed as she realized where she was staring. "Don't they have a size on them?" Assuming the most businesslike manner she could muster, she took the pants from him and inspected the faded label. "I think these are a thirty-four."

"I don't know what size I am," he told her, "but the ones I'm wearing are too small."

She could see that. They hugged him as if they'd been poured on, and the hems showed his ankles. "What size are they?"

"Dunno." He looked across his shoulder, then turned his back to her. "Have a look?"

The jeans weren't the only garment that was too small. His threadbare white T-shirt clung to his broad shoulders and outlined the muscles of his back all the way to the waistband of the jeans.

Hesitantly she slid a thumb into the band of the jeans and tried to peek at the label inside. He smelled of soap and faintly of male sweat. Surprisingly, she didn't find it offensive.

"I can't see it," she said. Her cheek brushed against his warm, hard back and she jerked hastily away.

His hand went to the front of the jeans and she heard the snap open, the zip slide down a little. "Try now."

This time she kept a few inches distance between them, and gingerly turned the band. "Thirty-two," she informed him, trying to sound brisk and as if she wasn't feeling odd little hot shivers down her spine. "Why don't you try these on? There's a fitting room at the back of the shop."

He turned, and she sternly kept her gaze away from the unfastened front snap, the tantalizing inch or so of opening. "Do you think I need to?"

"It's the only way to tell for sure."

"I guess." He held up the shirt he'd picked out. Gray and hardly worn. It could almost have passed for new, but was half the price. "What do you think of this?"

What did *she* think? Paige blinked at him from behind her glasses. "I think you'll look terrific in it." He'd have looked terrific in anything. Didn't he know that?

"Really?" The killer smile reappeared.

"Really." She tried to sound firm and knowledgeable, like a real salesperson. "Why don't you try this with it?"

She turned to the shelves, remembering a waistcoat she'd unpacked last week. The front was green silk with self-stripes, the back velvet, and she'd thought at the time how elegant it looked. It would show up his unusual eyes.

He looked at it dubiously, obviously a bit taken aback. "That?"

"This." She draped it over his arm. "It might have been made for you."

He laughed. "If you think that, I'll try it."

He was doing it to humor her, and she thought he had no intention of buying it.

But when he came out of the cubbyhole with its spotted wall mirror and tired orange curtain he placed all three items on the counter. "Okay," he said. "But the waistcoat will cost me a meal."

Not sure if he was joking, she looked anxiously at him, and saw he was smiling again. "For all three," she said primly, "I'll give you a discount." She knocked fifty cents off the price, and later surreptitiously made it up out of her pocket money.

The following week she was crouched awkwardly in the small shop window, arranging some china that had just arrived, when she looked up and found him staring in at her.

She dropped a cup and had to scramble to rescue it before replacing it on the display stand. When she emerged from the window and made to negotiate the tricky deep step from the raised window to the floor, he was standing there, holding out his hand for her to grasp.

She took it, and he steadied her as she reached the floor. Somehow he was holding both her hands, looking down at her, and she pulled them away, feeling a bit breathless. "Thank you."

"Did I give you a fright?" he asked.

"It's all right. I hadn't realized anyone was there."

"Is that your job—the window display?"

"Part of it." She was more nimble than the older ones and enjoyed the task. It gave her a buzz when her display lured someone into the shop.

The new jeans he wore looked good on him, and so did the maroon T-shirt tucked into them. They fitted snugly, without the strained look that suggested he'd grown out of those he'd been wearing last time. No matter what he wore, he had to be the sexiest real-live man she'd ever seen, easily beating into oblivion the pop star pinups on her bedroom wall.

"Can I help you?" she asked him, as she would any customer, but instead of warm and welcoming it came out starchy, almost prissy.

He grinned as if he thought it amusing. "You already have," he said.

"Really?"

"Guess you don't remember, but you sold me some stuff last week—clothes."

As if she'd forget! Paige thought. Didn't he know how stunning he was? She nodded. "I remember."

"I wanted to thank you," he said. "I wore them to a job interview, and…well, I got the job."

"Oh, that's cool!" She broke into a smile. "What kind of job?"

He was looking at her strangely, as if she'd just given him a small shock. Then he shrugged self-deprecatingly. "Only working in a café kitchen and they're not promising anything permanent, but…well, it's enough to keep the wolf happy." When she looked blank for a moment, he added, "The one that's howling at my door."

By then she'd got it anyway, but didn't say so, just smiled.

"And we get free food," he said.

Her heart sank a little. Still smiling, she queried, "We?" And then wondered if she'd been nosy.

"Me and the wolf," he explained. "That's one hungry critter."

She laughed then, and he looked pleased. It struck her that he'd been aiming for that, trying to make her laugh with the corny joke. The thought warmed her cheeks, and she told herself not to be silly. Why would a guy like him be the least bit interested in a girl like her? And especially the way she looked now, in her uniform and with no makeup, her hair tied in those girly pigtails, the only way to keep it tidy and out of her eyes at school.

It wasn't as though he were some pathetic old man with a fetish about schoolgirls. He couldn't be much older than she was. He'd like *pretty* girls who matched his own spectacular good looks. Blondes with bouncy curls, brunettes with flowing, glossy manes, or blazing redheads—girls who wore bright, shiny lipstick to outline their luscious mouths, who colored their eyelids with the exact shadow to enhance eyes that were a clear blue or green or soft, sexy brown, instead of an indeterminate greenish-brown flecked with splashes of blue and gold. Girls who didn't have to wear glasses. Not plain-Jane girls like Paige Camden.

But, amazingly, he was looking at her as though he liked her a lot. And even more amazingly, he said, "What time do you finish here? Can we grab a coffee together afterward?"

CHAPTER SIX

PAIGE stared at him openmouthed, no doubt looking like a particularly stupid goldfish. When she found her voice she squeaked, "Me?"

"Me and you." His smile faded. "I owe you. I'd like to buy you a coffee."

The funny little flutterings inside her subsided. "No, you don't. There's no need to buy me anything."

That was the first time she saw his stubborn look. He looked up, away from her, and his chin thrust out. His eyes when they returned to her were darkened and stormy. "I want to," he said. "It's a debt, and I always pay my debts."

He smiled again, and she knew she was supposed to sprinkle a grain or two of salt on the words. But the smile was irresistible. Even as it occurred to her that he probably used it all the time to get what he wanted, she gave in. Because whatever the reason, at the moment what he wanted was her...or at least some of her time, and even if it was only out of gratitude, the prospect was decidedly alluring.

"Five o'clock," she murmured. "I'll meet you outside."

When the shop closed up and the woman who sometimes dropped her off on her own way home

96

asked if she wanted a lift, she said, "Thanks, but I'm meeting someone."

And as the woman walked away Jager peeled himself away from the adjacent wall where he'd been lounging with his thumbs tucked into the pockets of his jeans, and came over to her, taking her hand.

His strong fingers closed around hers, and his eyes smiled, although his mouth stayed firm and straight. It was a wonderful mouth, she realized, fascinated by the clean outline of it, the indentation that softened the shape of his upper lip, the determined set of the lower one.

"What's your name?" Taking her with him, he started walking along the street. She had never held hands with a boy before, but he made it seem natural, comfortable and yet somehow exciting too.

"Paige," she answered him. "Paige Camden."

He repeated it, in a sexy undertone that made her toes tingle inside her regulation black lace-ups. "Paige. That's nice."

She was glad he thought so. "What's yours?"

"Jager." He spelled it out for her. "*J-a-g-e-r.*" She guessed he'd had to do it for lot of people. "Jeffries," he added. "JJ, if you like."

She liked "Jager." But she asked, "Is that what your friends call you? JJ?"

"I don't have friends." As if aware that he'd shocked her, he added, "Some of my workmates up north called me that."

"You come from up north?"

"Yep." He halted outside a coffee shop. The

aroma of coffee floated out to the pavement where a few tables had been set to augment those inside.

"Will this do?"

"It's fine." Whatever he suggested would have been fine with her. Already just being with him was enough.

They had two cups of coffee each and Jager asked where she lived, if she had brothers and sisters, and were her parents still together. He seemed interested when she talked about her family, her home.

"How long have you been in Auckland?" she asked, and he said a few months. He was living in a cheap boardinghouse, but now that he had a job he'd be finding something better.

Jager stirred crystals into his second coffee and looked at her rather probingly. "How old are you, Paige?"

"Sixteen."

His eyelids flickered. "You wouldn't lie to me, would you?"

"Why should I?"

For a moment he regarded her somberly. Then a faint smile curved his beautiful mouth. "Yeah, why should you?"

She realized what worried him. Sixteen was over the legal age of consent. A strange mix of sensations—shock, pleasure, anticipation and righteous anger—sizzled through her blood. She ducked her head to hide a blush.

"What are you doing at school?" Jager asked.

She chose to take that literally, and listed the subjects she was studying—English, history, art. She was in her last year and planned to attend university.

"You're a smart girl," he said. "That's young for university, isn't it?"

Uncomfortably she shrugged that off, hunching over her coffee. "I'll be seventeen." She was a conscientious student and, not being pretty or vivacious, had fewer distractions than some of her schoolmates. "What did you do up north?" she asked him.

He talked about his first job on a fishing boat, interweaving scary stories of storms and dangerous machinery with anecdotes about colorful characters and minor mishaps at sea that made her burst into laughter.

He grinned back at her appreciatively. "I like making you laugh," he told her, sounding almost surprised, and she looked down into her coffee cup again, embarrassed, making him laugh in turn.

"You're shy!" he accused, as if the discovery delighted him. And she raised her eyes and said, "I am not!" And then, "Well, yes, I am really. But it's not funny."

He reached over the table for her hand and held it tightly. "I don't mean to laugh at you, Paige."

She muttered, "It's all right." And tried to withdraw her hand, but he held it tighter.

"It's not all right if I hurt you," he insisted. He let her go then. "Hit me if you like."

Her gaze flew up to his. He looked quite serious. "I don't want to hit you!"

He smiled at her—not the sexy smile this time, but an almost tentative one. "Good. But if I'm ever out of line, feel free. Or just tell me what I've done wrong.''

She couldn't help the thrill that ran over her entire body. He'd offered her coffee, a thank-you gesture for a minor service. But now he was implying some kind of ongoing relationship.

"I don't hit people," she said. And then, because she was curious about him and also innately cautious and not a fool, she asked bluntly, "Do you?"

He shook his head. "Only if they hit me first. And never female people." He held her eyes. "Never."

She believed him. And her belief had not been misplaced. Even when they were tearing themselves and each other apart, when their ill-judged marriage was disastrously breaking up into shards of wounding words and bitter accusations, Jager had not once raised a hand to her.

When he lifted his hand now from its resting place on the couch back, it was to finger a strand of hair back from her cheek to behind her ear.

The movement startled her, and she stiffened.

"What are you thinking?" he said. "Should I be grateful that my old man suddenly remembered my existence?"

She didn't think gratitude was in his vocabulary. "You of all people should know everyone makes mistakes when they're young and...hormone-driven. He can't have been much older than you were when you...when we..."

"We got married," Jager said harshly. "There's a difference."

"Well, it turned out to be not such a hot idea," she reminded him.

"Yes." He got up rather suddenly. "If we start on that subject again…"

He was right. It could only lead to strife.

"Thanks again for your help." She followed him to the door.

"Anytime." He turned with his hand on the knob. "Anything. I mean that, Paige."

When he'd gone, the rooms with their newly gleaming floors seemed empty. She wandered through the house switching off lights and locking up, and found herself staring at her bed in the spare room and picturing Jager lying there against the pillows, waiting for her the way he had so often when they were married, hands behind his head, his magnificent chest bare as he watched her prepare to join him.

She'd been shy at first, and sometimes he'd taken pity and pretended to be absorbed in a book or magazine while she took off her clothes and donned a nightshirt or pajamas. But if she caught him peeking and scolded he'd laugh, then bound out of bed and catch her to him, smothering her protests with kisses, and take her back to the bed to complete undressing her himself.

Gradually she'd become less inhibited, even boldly, deliberately teasing him, treating him to their own private strip show. She knew her face could never compete with the girls he might have had, but her body was fine. At least it had never failed to arouse him.

He'd told her once, when they were lying close after making love, that the day he walked into the shop and saw her on the ladder, with her uniform hiked up her thighs as she reached for the vase on the top shelf, he'd wanted to drag her down and into his arms right then and there.

Half-mortified, half-delighted, she said, "You were looking up my skirt!"

"Couldn't help it," he said, smiling wickedly. "I thought, *Wow, great legs.* Then I started wondering what the rest of you looked like under that skirt and sweater."

"You did?" She'd have been horrified if she'd known what he was thinking.

"Until you came down and the penny dropped. You were wearing a uniform. I thought, Hell, a schoolgirl."

"Not, *Hell, the face doesn't live up to the legs?*"

"Don't be silly." He pinched her nose, and dropped a kiss on her mouth. "You've got a great face."

It was nice of him to say so, but she hadn't believed his offhand compliment. She was just grateful that he never reminded her she was no beauty.

The way he made love to her made her feel beautiful. He worshiped her body with his, just as it said in the marriage service. Inexperienced though she was, it hadn't been long before she matched his passion and his dedication to their mutual pleasure.

And when he buried his face against her neck and moaned his fulfillment, his arms wrapped around her, his thighs snug in the sweet cradle of hers, it didn't matter what she looked like. At that moment he was wholly given over to sensation, to the satisfaction of the need she'd created with her body.

And thinking about it so many years later, created a tension in her that she tried to shake off, moving briskly to get herself into bed—alone.

She'd bought a queen-size bed simply because she was used to it and no longer comfortable in a single one. She had no intention of sharing it with anyone, but for the first time it occurred to her that it was a big bed for one person. Lying there, she was conscious of the empty space beside her.

Irritated with herself, she plumped the pillows against the headboard, right in the middle, and reached for a book. But the story didn't hold her, and she sighed, letting the book drop to the floor, and switched off the light.

A pukeko screeched forlornly somewhere down by the beach. The birds had adapted to city life remarkably well—she'd seen them stalking on their long red legs right beside the busy motorway, undeterred by traffic roaring by. Faintly she could hear the water lapping on the shore. A lone morepork called from one of the neighbors' trees.

She was lonely. In the darkness she admitted it to herself. Over the past few weeks she'd had company almost every waking hour. Being with Maddie and Glen—and Jager—had helped her stave off the emptiness that lay in wait.

But it hadn't gone away.

She wondered if it ever would.

* * *

"Maddie tells me you've been working hard on your new home." Her mother had phoned her at work. "And Glen," Margaret added with an air of surprise.

"Glen's been a great help," Paige agreed. Had Maddie mentioned that Jager had pitched in too? Either she'd kept quiet about it or her mother preferred to ignore the fact.

"We haven't seen much of you."

Paige swallowed a pang of guilt, reminding herself that her parents knew they were welcome to visit her anytime.

"Why don't you come for dinner tonight?" Margaret said brightly.

Paige had been looking forward to an evening poring over wallpaper samples she'd picked up that day, but she said, "That would be nice."

"Good. We'll see you after work, then."

Paige arrived with a French loaf and a bottle of wine, which her mother assured her was welcome, if unnecessary.

After freshening up and shedding the jacket she'd been wearing with her ruby-red skirt and cream blouse, Paige entered the big formal sitting room where her father waited. He kissed her cheek and introduced her to a man who had risen at her entrance, putting down the glass in his hand.

He was solidly built and in his mid-thirties, a smooth-skinned executive type with a firm handshake and a direct stare behind authoritative horn-rims. "Philip is our new head of accounting," Henry said. "We've been talking over some of his projected strategies for the company. My daughter, Paige."

Philip was pleased to meet her, or so he said. Paige's antenna went up. Had her mother just wanted to even up the numbers at the table? Or was this a setup?

Over dinner she seized the opportunity when it arose of asking if he had a family.

Philip adjusted his glasses. "A boy who's ten, and a little girl, six. They live with their mother. We're divorced."

"I'm sorry."

"It's a couple of years now. One must go on."

Margaret said, mixing approval with understanding, "We can't live in the past." She glanced blandly at Paige. "Paige's husband died in America, you know. She's come home to start over."

Paige speared a piece of delicately grilled fish with unnecessary force. She was surprised at her mother. She'd have thought Margaret would expect her to observe a proper period of mourning for her husband before even thinking about other men.

Philip said quietly, "I'm very sorry, Paige."

Responding to the genuine sympathy, she said, "Thank you." It wasn't his fault that her parents thought he'd be good for her.

After dinner Paige showed her mother some of her wallpaper samples while the men talked business. Margaret went to make more coffee, declining Paige's help, and Philip strolled over to take her place on the sofa beside Paige. "You're redecorating?" he asked.

Surprisingly, he was an ardent do-it-yourselfer, with plenty of useful advice. When Margaret came back with the coffee he made to get up, but she gave him a pleased smile and told him not to move.

Paige left as soon as she decently could, though not before she'd been maneuvered into inviting Philip to call at the cottage and see for himself what she was doing with it.

At least she'd managed to avoid an actual date and time, leaving the invitation vague.

The following Saturday Paige rose early and prepared to hang wallpaper. Maddie and Glen were away for the weekend attending a friend's wedding in Taranaki, and Paige had assured them blithely that she could manage on her own. Anyway, she didn't want to monopolize all of Glen's weekends, knowing that Maddie didn't share his enthusiasm.

And she hadn't heard from Jager.

But when, a half hour after she'd hung the first drop in the sitting room, she heard a car stop outside, followed by a knock on the front door, her heart did a little skip as she called from her perch on a stepladder, "Come in." She'd left it on the latch after collecting the morning paper. Just in case, she'd told herself, without completing the thought. Just in case Jager arrived while she was unable to answer the door.

She heard it open tentatively, and a man's voice said, "Paige?"

Then Philip appeared in the sitting room doorway, his horn-rims turned enquiringly up to her. He was casually dressed and she supposed in his way he was quite good-looking. But he wasn't Jager.

To cover her sickening disappointment she gave

him a hugely welcoming smile. "Philip! How nice of you to drop in. Just a minute…"

"Don't move. Carry on." He crossed the room and stood with one hand on the ladder, just by her knees. "You're doing well," he told her. "And using paste too," he added approvingly. He'd told her even pre-pasted paper hung better with it. "But it'll be easier with two of us."

He was right. The work went much faster, and he was very good at managing the tricky bits about the doors and windows.

He was smoothing an intricately cut piece around the old tiled fireplace while Paige brushed paste onto the next drop when there was another knock on the door, a decisive double rap.

"Excuse me." She left the long strip of paper on the trestle table and hurried into the hallway. Jager was already pushing the door wide. It had probably opened when he knocked.

He stepped in, latching the door behind him, and scowled at her. "What's the use of having a burglar alarm if you're going to leave your damned door open?" he demanded.

"It's broad daylight, and I thought—"

"*I* thought you'd have had more sense. It might have been all right with Glen and me here, but when you're on your own—"

"I'm not."

That stopped him. "I thought the car outside belonged to the neighbors."

"You'd better come in," she said, despite the fact that he was already in, "and meet Philip." She turned and went back to the sitting room, leaving him to follow. "I can't leave what I'm doing."

"Who the hell is…?"

Philip put down the smoothing brush in his hand and straightened. Somehow he suddenly looked bigger, his chest deeper, his shoulders broader, although he couldn't match Jager's height. Like a puffer fish, Paige thought bemusedly, swelling to a larger size when threatened. Behind the glasses his eyes surveyed the invader with cool assessment. "That'd be me," he said mildly, but despite the thunder in Jager's gaze he wasn't intimidated.

Aware that the testosterone level in the room had just doubled—at least—Paige refrained from fanning a hand before her face, and introduced them.

When Philip stepped forward with his hand outstretched she almost expected the two of them to engage in arm-wrestling, but Jager merely gripped the other man's hand cursorily and then dropped it. His expression had become shuttered, only the narrowed gleam of his eyes indicating any emotion at all.

He cast a glance at the walls, then looked back at Philip. "You're a professional?" he asked. "Paige hired you…"

"Philip's a friend." Paige hoped he didn't mind being claimed as such when they barely knew each other. "He kindly offered to help."

"I told you, if you needed any more help—"

"He's experienced."

The gleam under Jager's black lashes altered slightly. "Is that so?" He looked at Paige. His gaze dropped over the paint-stained shirt that nearly covered the old shorts she wore with it, lingering on her legs before returning in leisurely fashion to her face. "I have some experience too," he said, sparing a glance for the other man. "Paige and I have been working on it for a while."

Philip wasn't stupid. His alert eyes went from Jager to Paige, and she said hurriedly, "My sister's husband brought Jager along to help. They're half brothers."

"So you're kind of related," Philip said, sorting that out, "by marriage."

Jager agreed, "You could say that." Paige felt the sting of his glance, but refused to meet it.

He looked around the room again. "You've been busy." Returning his gaze to Philip, he asked, "Been here long?"

Philip looked down at his watch, but before he could answer Paige said, "We've come a long way in a short time. Philip doesn't mess about."

The stormy green eyes lighted on her again. "I'm beginning to think that's what I've been doing."

Meeting his direct, gloves-off gaze, she said steadily, "You were very useful." Then recklessly she added, "All that male muscle was great. Now I'm into a different phase—Philip offered his skills and he's teaching me a lot."

For an instant longer he held her eyes, then he switched his attention to Philip. "You a teacher, Phil?"

Philip laid his elbow on a step of the ladder. "I'm an accountant...Jay."

Jager showed his teeth, but Paige wasn't certain the gesture could be called a smile. "A numbers man, huh? So how does an accountant get experience at…ah…home decorating?'' He made it sound like needlepoint.

Philip answered equably, ''My wife and I renovated three homes during our marriage.''

''Uh-huh.'' Jager cocked his head, hands thrust into the pockets of his cotton casuals. ''None of them satisfied you for long?''

''We sold them for good money and moved on.''

''Is that what you do? Move on?''

Philip smiled. ''We got a better house each time.''

''You and your wife.'' Jager rocked slightly on his heels. ''Uh…you're not married anymore?''

''No.'' A hint of regret colored Philip's tone. ''She's selling real estate now, doing pretty well.''

Jager's head tilted, as if he were sniffing the air for a foreign scent. He said, ''And you…do you have your own practice?''

Philip stopped leaning on the ladder and adopted the same stance as Jager, his hands sliding into his pockets. ''I'm head of accounting at Camden Industries,'' he said.

Jager too, looked at Paige before returning his gaze to Philip. He hadn't moved, but she was sure every one of his formidable muscles had tightened, as if he were a tiger ready to spring. *''Camden's.''*

Paige could see his mind was working, probably overheating. Making two and two into at least five and a half. His quick glance stung her with contemptuous accusation. ''So,'' he said to Philip, ''you work for Paige's daddy.''

Philip's jaw jutted. "I work for the firm. Paige and I met at Henry's house."

Paige didn't blame him for rising to Jager's bait. But he couldn't know that Jager had never been invited to use her father's first name, that he'd always meticulously called her parents Mr. and Mrs. Camden.

Taking advantage of the small silence that ensued, Philip asked Jager, "What do you do?"

His expression altered when Jager told him. Evidently he'd heard of JJ Communications. "You're *that* Jeffries?" he queried. "I thought you'd be older."

"I'm old enough."

"Married?" Philip didn't sound hopeful.

Jager's mocking gaze slid to Paige. "Not anymore."

She'd had enough of this. "You can see," she told Jager, "we're busy right now. I have to finish this before it dries." She picked up her abandoned brush and dipped it into the paste. "So unless you've come to help with the *home decorating*..." She let her gaze stray pointedly to the door.

His faint grin acknowledged the jibe she'd turned back on him.

Calling her bluff, he said, "Did you think I'd leave this without seeing it through? You know me better than that, Paige."

Paige's mouth tightened. Her brush slapped paste onto the back of the paper. She was aware of Philip's curious stare before he turned to shift the stepladder to a new position. She said, "Philip thinks we should have done the walls before the floors.'' She was, she realized, brandishing Philip at him like a shield.

''Does he?'' Jager was standing by her now, and he leaned over and moved the piece of paper to allow her to reach the end. His tone implied that he didn't give a damn what Philip thought.

She carried the wet, sticky strip over to Philip and he ascended the ladder to align the paper carefully at the top and began smoothing it down with the wide brush Paige handed to him.

Behind her she sensed Jager quietly steaming as she helped Philip adjust the edges.

When she turned, Jager had the next piece ready.

''I have some experience too,'' he said. ''Remember?''

His laser gaze and raised brows brought it all back. The dingy one-room ''studio flat'' they'd rented because it was all they could afford, with the landlord's grudging permission to redecorate, but at their own expense. They'd bought paint at a sale and started by slapping color on the tiny kitchen.

It had looked so good they'd become ambitious and found some cheap, cheerful paper to cover the other walls.

Given the quality of the paper and their own ignorance, maybe they hadn't made too bad a job of it but, ''I don't think that counts,'' she said quellingly.

Jager folded the paper and carried it over to Philip. ''We all learn from our mistakes,'' he said.

CHAPTER SEVEN

THE men appeared to have called a truce. When Philip began flexing his arms and grimacing at their stiffness, Jager took his turn on the ladder.

By the day's end they were working in tandem, exchanging male banter with a slight edge, and Paige felt like snapping someone's head off. Somehow she'd been shouldered out to the role of the Little Woman who provided tea and biscuits and rustled up lunch, handed smoothing brushes and trimming knives when they were needed, and was sometimes allowed to put paste on, but couldn't be trusted with anything important like climbing ladders or actually hanging the paper.

Unfair. The two of them were certainly getting through the job more quickly than she would have on her own, hardly pausing to eat, although they gratefully downed the drinks she made at frequent intervals. They seemed to be in competition to see who could work faster, longer, harder, an element of driving determination that had been absent when Glen and Jager worked together.

They finished the sitting room and a bedroom, then surveyed the hallway, smaller but tricky because of the doorways leading off it.

Paige decided to assert herself. "I'm tired," she announced truthfully, although her weariness had less to do with physical effort than coping with the palpable tension in the air. "And the light in here isn't very good. Thanks, guys, but let's leave it for tonight and I'll make you some dinner."

She thought there was a flicker of relief in Philip's expression. He took off his glasses and wiped the back of his hand across his forehead.

Jager cast her a searching look. "No need for you to cook for us. You'd better have an early night." He clapped a hand on Philip's shoulder and Paige thought she saw the other man control a wince. "Come on, Phil. We'll get out of here and let the lady rest, hmm?"

Since Paige wasn't arguing, Philip had to tacitly agree, his at first mulish stare becoming a rueful smile as he sketched a salute in Jager's direction, conceding him the point.

Paige kept her mouth shut, quietly seething. She wasn't about to throw herself between any swords. Or to make Philip an unwitting weapon, not even to give Jager the comeuppance that he richly deserved.

Somehow amid collecting jackets and saying their goodbyes, Jager managed to maneuver Philip out the door and send him down the steps first. Which allowed him to take a step back and say to Paige, "Make sure you get something to eat, yourself. Even if it's only a sandwich."

Not waiting for her to reply, he dipped his head and kissed her mouth, so briefly she had no chance to evade or respond. "See you tomorrow." And then he was bounding down the steps, jacket slung over his shoulder, to where Philip stood.

*   *   *

Philip too, had promised to return in the morning, but Jager arrived first.

Paige led him straight to the kitchen where she was making coffee. "You're early."

"You're up," he pointed out.

She picked up the toast she'd been eating. "Have you had breakfast?"

"Yeah. Is that all you're having?"

"It's all I need."

He ran his gaze over her old T-shirt and denim cutoffs. "That's open to argument."

"I'm not thin!"

His eyes were bland as they returned to her face. "I have no complaints about your figure, honey."

Exasperated, she turned her back on him to fiddle with the percolator.

He was leaning on the kitchen counter with a cup of coffee in his hand when she let Philip in later.

"I have to leave by lunchtime," Philip was telling her. "My w...ex-wife asked me to take the kids while she studies. She's getting herself a law degree." He sounded half-puzzled, half-proud. Seeing Jager, he nodded a wary greeting. "'Morning."

"You have kids?" Jager asked. Although he hadn't moved from his relaxed position, Paige sensed an undercurrent in the casual query.

"A boy and a girl," she remembered, bringing Jager's gaze to her face. "You didn't need to come today, Philip."

She couldn't read the oddly intent stare Jager gave her before he looked back at Philip. "We'd hate to take you away from your family," he said.

Even as Paige bridled at the possessive "we" Philip gave him a knowing grin. "Yeah, I know. But I've got all morning. And I don't like leaving anything halfway."

"Neither do I." Jager held the other man's gaze for a moment, then drained his cup. "And even though I was here before you, I guess I've been wasting time."

They had the hallway done before Philip left, apologizing again.

Paige shook her head. "You've been a huge help. I owe you. Why don't you come for dinner some time? Bring the children and we'll take them down to the beach for a swim."

He looked pleased. "Well, thanks. I may take you up on that."

Paige closed the door as he left, and turned to find Jager regarding her from the kitchen doorway, his shoulder propped against the frame. As she walked toward him he didn't move. "That's a step isn't it?" he said. "Inviting him to bring his kids. Have you met them?"

"No." She had to stop in front of him. He looked big and formidable. Telling him she hardly knew Philip was suddenly not an option. She had an overwhelming sensation of being gathered into the powerful male aura of Jager's sexuality, with scant hope of escape. Making a feeble effort at self-defense, she tilted her chin and said, "Not yet."

A muscle along his jaw tightened. The warning

glitter in his eyes made her heart thud. "Do you want children?"

The blunt question startled her. "Aidan and I hoped for a baby...but it never happened."

Her eyes stung and she bit on her lip to stop the tears. She'd thought she was all cried out for Aidan, and it was humiliating to be weeping for him in front of Jager.

His black brows had drawn together. He straightened away from the doorway, swearing under his breath, and took her arm to guide her into the kitchen where he pulled a chair from the table. "Sit down," he growled, almost forcing her to do so.

As if that would help. He'd never had any idea what to do with a weeping woman. Not that she'd done it often, preferring to keep her tears private.

She gulped down a sob, and gave a spurt of shaky laughter. "I'm all right."

"Sure." The bite in his voice was savage. "Can I get you a coffee? Or something stronger?"

"Coffee would be nice." She sat up, removed her glasses and pushed a few strands of hair from her face, brushing the incipient tears away in the same movement before replacing the glasses firmly on her nose.

She watched Jager make the coffee and find bread, butter, cheese and spreads. He added a pack of sliced ham, gave her a plate and knife, then poured the coffee and set a mug before her.

"Eat," he said, pulling up a chair himself.

When they had both done so he made more coffee

and sat again, pushing aside his empty plate to wrap his fingers around the mug he'd chosen. He seemed to be gripping it tightly despite the hot liquid inside, and his voice was deep and even when he said, "Tell me about Aidan."

Paige had begun to lift her own cup, but she put it down again so quickly a few drops spilled on the table. The surface coating was impermeable, but Jager silently got up and found a sponge, wiping up the spill before tossing the sponge into the sink. Then he resumed his seat and waited.

Paige glanced at him. He looked purposeful and intent and, except for a certain rigidity in his face, almost sympathetic. "Aidan," she said huskily, staring down at her coffee, "was a wonderful husband. A great person."

She fancied she heard Jager's teeth come together. "You met him in America?" His voice was gritty but carefully expressionless.

"Yes." Her parents had sent her there to visit her aunt and uncle who had settled in Pennsylvania, and to get to know her cousins, they said.

Of course it was really to help her recover from the debacle of her marriage. Which they'd insisted had been no real marriage at all, since Jager had falsified both their ages on the license application.

Despite their lack of consent, they had discovered—to Henry's chagrin and Margaret's horror—the bare civil ceremony was legally binding. Probably only the prospect of having a son-in-law with a criminal record had deterred Henry from making good his threat to have Jager jailed for making a false declaration.

"Aidan was a friend of my cousins. He was kind, when I needed kindness."

Once she had admitted to her parents that they were right, she *had* been too young to know what she was doing, it had been all too easy to slide back into letting them make the decisions. When her father brought her the divorce papers his lawyer had drawn up, she recoiled, but his patient reasoning wore her down, and she signed the document with shaking fingers before running to her room, where she'd wept into her lonely pillow all night.

"It won't be final for two years," Henry had warned her, not knowing that her stupid heart found that faintly hopeful. "But you'll be a free woman before you're twenty."

They had been supportive and understanding when she arrived tearfully on the doorstep and announced that her marriage was over. And not once had they said "We told you so." They enfolded her in warm love and sympathy, and with calm words of wisdom they had strengthened her resolve to separate herself from Jager and the roller coaster of their emotional life. And, noting her sensitivity on the subject, they had mostly refrained, with occasionally visible difficulty, from overtly criticizing him.

Overwhelmingly grateful, she'd begun, guiltily, to feel stifled by affection when her mother said her aunt in America would love to have her stay. And didn't she think that was what she needed? Her uncle, a college lecturer, would help get her a student visa. She could make up for some of her missed schooling.

Her very panic at the thought of leaving the country that held Jager told Paige it *was* what she needed. To get right away...away from the temptation to go flying back into his arms, back to the cycle of wild happiness and crushed hopes, of amazing, spontaneous sex and its aftermath of exhausted euphoria—and of heated, door-slamming, raised-voice quarrels that usually ended in bed with more sex, but left a legacy of simmering bitterness and an increasing, gnawing sense that nothing had really been resolved.

"Weren't your cousins kind?" Jager asked, digging a spoon into the sugar bowl on the table, although he didn't take sugar.

"Yes, they were nice." She watched him moodily lift the spoon and dig it in again. "And they were fun."

It was like living in an alternative universe where her runaway marriage had never happened. Where she'd never met a boy named Jager, never fallen madly in love, never defied her parents to be with him. Never finally admitted defeat.

She had hidden alternating bouts of despair and a bewildering, unfocused rage behind a brittle facade of feverish enjoyment, filled her days with new things, new activities and new people and, when she wasn't studying or discovering America, partied to the max with her cousins and their friends. It gave her less time to think. Less time to remember...to wish that things had turned out differently.

Sometimes she'd almost forgotten the aching void

deep down inside her. She paused to sip some coffee. "Aidan was part of a group my cousins and I used to go around with."

Jager stopped digging holes in the sugar and sat back, a hand hooking into his belt. "Was he good-looking?"

She couldn't help a slight smile. What did it matter? "He was nice-looking." Not like Jager, who would stand out in any company. She had scarcely noticed Aidan until the night she'd found herself standing alone in a corner at a party, while all about her people were drinking, laughing, dancing with their arms around each other.

She'd been attacked by a wave of longing. Longing for Jager, for his arms around her, his cheek against her temple, his thighs warming hers as they swayed in time to the music.

Holding a half-empty glass, she tried to stop tears from flowing down her cheeks, wondering what the hell she was doing in a strange land when everything she cared about was half a world away. And knowing it didn't make any difference, because Jager didn't love her anymore—he never had really loved her.

Aidan's hand touched her arm, and his gentle voice asked, "D'you want to dance, Paige?"

Unable to speak, she'd simply shaken her head, and he'd peered down into her face and said, "Let's go outside."

He shifted his hand to her waist and steered her to the door, and when they reached the quiet, tree-lined street he silently took her hand, and they walked like that for a long time.

"He had a gift of empathy," she said. "He always seemed to know what to do. Or when to do nothing. Say nothing."

"That's a talent." Jager's voice was dry but when she looked up, alert for signs of irony, his expression was sober.

"He was a special person," she said. "Everyone liked him."

"And you loved him."

"Yes, I did." She looked up at him, her eyes sad and clear. "I was lucky to be his wife."

It hadn't been the heedless, all-consuming emotion that burned so fiercely for Jager. But she'd valued the paler, steadier flame that she'd thought would last a lifetime. Until it was cruelly, abruptly snuffed out.

She sensed a leashed anger in Jager's tightened jaw and the flash of fire in his eyes. He turned his head and stared out the window, where the top of a ponga fern waved its lacy fronds in a breeze off the sea. His profile was strong and austere. It struck her again how very grown-up he looked now.

His eyes still on the window, he ground out, "I'm glad you were happy."

Tentatively she said, "What about you? Did you...? Have you been happy?"

"I've been busy. Too busy to think about it." He pushed his chair back and stood up. "If you want the rest of the papering done today..."

This time she got to do some of the real work. When they hung the last strip of silk-look gold paper in her bedroom, Jager swung her down from the ladder to the floor with his hands on her waist. "That's it. We're all done."

"It looks great. Thank you." She edged away from his hold, forgetting they'd moved the bed into the middle of the room to clear the walls. It caught the back of her legs and she fell onto the soft cover.

She saw the awareness in Jager's eyes, and held her breath as he stepped forward. But he only took her hand to help her up and a second later she was standing again.

"Do you want something to eat?" she asked to break the silence that followed. It was getting late and they hadn't eaten, intent on getting the job finished.

He released her. "If you're not too tired we could go out for a meal."

"Then I'm paying."

"Uh-uh." He shook his head.

"It's only fair."

"Too bad."

She knew that look. Argument, however rational, would only rebound off the rock wall of his stubborn will.

"We'll stay here then," she said, "and I'll make something."

The pugnacious thrust of his jaw showed his frustration, but all he said was, "I'll help."

She found a packet of pork strips in the freezer and thawed them in the microwave oven, and while she made a sweet-and-sour sauce and boiled a pot of rice Jager stir-fried vegetables.

They worked efficiently together, falling into a

rhythm established long ago, automatically moving aside to make room for each other.

Paige hadn't realized she was hungry, but she ate with relish, while Jager cleaned up an amount that would have done her for days.

She had asked him to open a bottle of wine, but noticed that like her he'd drunk sparingly. After they'd pushed aside their empty plates there was still some left in the bottle.

When she offered it to Jager he said, "I'm driving." Then he looked directly at her. "Unless you'd like me to stay."

She met his eyes and they were quite serious, probing hers.

It occurred to her that she *would* like him to stay, to take her to bed and make love to her, give her the gift of forgetfulness for one night, and be there in the morning when she woke.

She saw that he'd read her face, saw the triumphant leap of hope in his eyes. Then she remembered the last time he had woken in her bed, at her parents' house. It hadn't solved anything.

"No," she said.

The hope was replaced by a hard accusation. "What changed your mind?"

Paige stiffened. "I haven't changed my mind. I'm not interested."

He said softly, "Don't lie to me, Paige. I know you too well."

"You knew the stupid little teenager who nearly ruined her life for you. You don't know the person I am now at all."

"Nearly ruined your life?" he repeated slowly.

"I gave up everything for you. My schooling, my family, my home..."

She hadn't realized how hard it would be.

Her father had refused to finance her studies while she insisted on staying with Jager, and although both parents had assured her she was welcome at home anytime, they wouldn't extend the invitation to her husband. Paige wouldn't visit without him, and of course they hadn't ever set foot in the dingy rented flat.

She inquired about a student loan but it wasn't enough to live on, and the amount she was going to owe by the time she had a degree was frightening.

Instead she got a job, assuring Jager that university had been her parents' plan, not hers. She didn't care as long as she could be with him.

"You said it was worth it," Jager reminded her. She had said so, determined to lie on the bed she'd made for herself, and when she shared it with Jager it did seem worth it.

For a while she hardly noticed how little money they had, although Jager had warned her he wasn't making much as a kitchen hand, and she'd conscientiously shopped for cheap cuts of meat and bargain vegetables to make their meals, even enjoying the challenge. Then he'd been promoted to barman and they'd celebrated by going out to dinner, the first time since their marriage.

And only a few weeks later he was sacked because he hadn't held onto his temper when an obnoxious customer became abusive.

Paige understood that his self-esteem couldn't withstand the man's malicious insults, but the sinking fear in her stomach wouldn't go away. The money she earned as a junior bookshop assistant would have to stretch far to keep them both. She economized further on meat and fish and cooked a lot of rice and pasta.

Sometimes she met her mother for a quick lunch in town, but as Margaret spent the time gently and insistently trying to ''make her see sense'' they were tense occasions, only adding to the estrangement. Her father phoned occasionally to gruffly inquire after her welfare, and she said she was fine.

She had never told them Jager was unemployed again.

Desperate, Paige answered an advertisement for nightclub dancers, promising good money but ''No experience necessary'' and was turned down. Her face, they told her bluntly, didn't match up to her figure. She wished she'd thought to leave her glasses behind and put on makeup, but it probably wouldn't have made any difference.

Jager found the newspaper where she'd ringed the ad, and she tried to make an amusing story of the interview. Only he didn't think it was funny. White-faced and furious, he'd told her he wasn't going to have her selling her damn body for him. And out of a simmering resentment she hadn't known was there, she'd retaliated that it wouldn't be necessary if he'd been less touchy about his stupid pride.

They made up later with frenzied lovemaking, both of them determined to close the frightening rift they'd revealed. *It's all right,* they'd told each other. *I didn't mean it. I'm sorry.*

Jager obtained temporary work laboring on a building site.

The day he came home lugging a secondhand computer, they had another row.

He put the machine down on the tiny kitchen table and Paige exclaimed, shocked into shrillness, "What on earth are we going to do with a computer?"

Accustomed to a home where the dishes went into a dishwasher, the washing machine and dryer worked perfectly, the hot water never ran out and she had no idea what the electricity bill came to, she'd been struggling to accustom herself to hand-washing dishes, dealing with an ancient and pernickety coin-operated communal washing machine, and saving money by drying clothes on a sagging outside wire in a cold, overgrown yard.

She hadn't had anything new to wear since she'd moved out of her parents' home, and earlier that day had yearned wistfully at a pretty skirt in a shop window and known there was no way she could justify buying it.

A computer seemed an indulgence, a luxury they couldn't afford.

"I'm not working for other people all my life," Jager said. "This could be my ticket to my own business."

"You dropped out of school!" she reminded him, unable to erase the scorn from her voice. "And what do you know about business?"

He'd become defensive and angry. "So I didn't

have a rich daddy to send me to a fancy private school—'' he sneered ''—and I left when I knew they couldn't teach me any more than I could learn off my own bat. But I'm not stupid. I'll learn.''

He had, and proved her wrong in the end. But she'd doubted him that night, and he'd lashed out in return. The wounds had never quite healed.

Throughout their short marriage she resented the computer almost as if it were another woman. She didn't understand the complex calculations he made on it for a digital communication system that he said was an improvement on anything on the market.

She knew he was smart and could probably have equaled or even surpassed her own exam results if he'd stayed at school. But she also knew that his youth and lack of qualifications, experience or contacts would make it difficult for him to succeed in business.

''Your parents could have made it easier on you.'' Jager's hand closed around his empty wineglass.

''They were doing what they thought best for me.''

''You still believe that?'' Hostility glittered in his eyes.

''Jager, I was seventeen. Far too young for marriage. Can you blame them?''

At the time Jager had wanted to try to talk them into giving consent.

''They'll stop us,'' she'd told him, alarmed at the thought. ''We can't tell them. Not until we're married.''

She'd told them she was spending the weekend

with a friend's family at their beach cottage. Lying to them felt wrong, but marrying Jager felt so right, and this was the only way. They'd been married quickly and quietly on Friday afternoon, and spent two magical nights and days together in a seaside motel they could ill afford.

She kept the secret until after her final high school exams, seeing Jager whenever she could, both of them frustrated by the constraints on their privacy, their time together. Then, having finished school, she announced that she wanted to live with her husband. And all hell broke loose.

She'd expected it, of course. But not that her parents would be so inflexible. With the optimism of youth she had thought that, presented with a fait accompli, after the initial shock they would accept Jager as the man she intended to spend her life with.

She hadn't been prepared for the suspicion and hostility they held toward him. Most of it she could brush off, but some things stuck, worming their way into her mind, her heart. Her mother saying bitterly, ''He took one look at you and saw easy money—or so he thought. A rich man's daughter.''

Paige had flared in his defense. ''He didn't have any idea who I was! Or who my father was.''

Margaret snorted. ''Everyone knows the school uniform.''

''Not all the pupils are from wealthy families.'' But people did tend to assume it. And she'd told Jager on that very first date what her father did, what his company was.

She despised herself for making an opportunity to ask Jager later if he'd recognized the uniform.

"Didn't have a clue," he'd answered. "I hadn't been in Auckland for long then. Why?"

"I just wondered." And then she felt guilty for lying to him.

Her father claimed angrily that Jager had asked him for money, and threatened him when he refused. She'd said she didn't believe that, and hung up on him. But her father wasn't a liar.

"I asked him for a loan," Jager admitted. "To help develop my ideas into a business, because the banks won't touch it without collateral and I thought for your sake he might. I drew up an agreement, with interest and everything. I'd have paid him back."

"You didn't mention it to me!"

"I wasn't going to tell you if he turned me down. I did it for you, Paige. Because you deserve better than this place, this life." He looked around the little flat, the meager furnishings.

She could imagine how much pride he had needed to swallow even to ask.

Jager said bitterly, "He wouldn't even look at the proposal. He'd rather see me drown, and take you with me. That's how much he loves his daughter!"

"He said you threatened him."

Jager frowned. "Things got a bit heated. I don't remember all the details. He accused me of using you to extort money from him. I told him what sort of a father I thought he was, and that he'd lose you completely the way he was carrying on."

Two versions. She believed Jager, of course she did. It was a misunderstanding.

But the misunderstandings proliferated, even after he landed a job with an electronics company, with better pay and better prospects. Perhaps by then it had been too late. She couldn't remember now what the final row had been about. Something unimportant, probably, but the last straw. She'd packed a bag and walked out with tears streaming down her face and fogging her glasses, and flagged down a cab to take her home.

CHAPTER EIGHT

JAGER pushed back his chair but didn't get up. "Did your parents approve of Aidan?"

"They liked him. I told you—"

"Oh, yeah. Everybody did. And it goes without saying they like Philip. Are you prepared to take second place to his ex-wife and his children? He hasn't cut loose from her…emotionally." Jager's expression was ruthless.

"I don't care!" she said, exasperated.

Fleetingly he looked furious, before his face went totally blank.

This was pointless. "I hardly know him!" Paige said, angry herself. "I met him at my parents' place and he offered me help with the decorating. He's just a nice man."

Jager was skeptical. "And he hopes you can help him get over his broken marriage. Not to mention it can't do his career any damage if he marries the boss's daughter."

"Not everyone has your eye for the main chance."

His head jerked back. "What?"

"Why did *you* really want to marry me? It certainly wasn't for my pretty face."

For once he appeared at a loss for words. "Why the hell do you think?" he demanded at last. "I was in love with you, dammit! I thought you were in love with me!''

''Would you have been so keen if my family hadn't had money?'' The tormenting suspicion that she'd denied even to herself, buried deep in her subconscious out of fear and pride and wilful refusal to recognize the possibility, finally broke to the surface in all its stark ugliness.

For an instant he looked utterly blank, then almost murderous, before he wiped that expression too, from his face, and said in a deadly tone, ''Would *you* have been so keen if I hadn't represented forbidden fruit? The bad boy from the wrong side of the tracks, the wrong side of the blanket? Your very own teenage rebellion? Well, it didn't last long once reality sank in, did it? When the going gets tough the rich little girls run back to Daddy.''

''That's not fair!''

''What's fair?'' he scoffed. ''*Life* isn't fair, Paige. The way I feel about you isn't *fair!* Nothing in this whole damn wide world is *fair*. This—'' he swooped to haul her from the chair and into his arms, the raging passion in his eyes making her gasp ''—isn't fair.'' And then his mouth crushed hers, with the same bewildering mix of anger and desire.

She could hardly breathe, he held her so close, and his warmth and his scent, sexy and seductive, drowned her in sensation. Her parted lips accepted the thrust of his tongue, and the taste of him was exciting beyond bearing.

He was instantly aroused, letting her know it with the closeness of his hold, the explicit nudging of his body against hers. The blood in her veins raced, heating her skin, making her dizzy.

She loved him, had always loved him. Everything, everyone else in the world became a distant, unreal memory. This was what she was born for, what she had once known and had given up for a half-life, for a pale imitation.

She strained against him, yearning even closer, and felt a tremor run through his entire body. He broke the kiss and stared down at her flushed face, her glazed eyes, his own as brilliant as polished emeralds. With shaking hands he cupped her face, tipping back her head, and dropped hot, fierce kisses down the line of her throat.

''The hell with this,'' he muttered, and kissed her again, too swiftly. He swung her into his arms and strode through to the bedroom where a high full moon shone through the window and in the uneven light his face took on mysterious planes and shadows, gaunt and proud and taut, like a warrior going into battle.

Then they were lying on the bed, and he hauled off her shirt, and tore his own from his body. ''I'm not offering you marriage this time,'' he said, the words grinding from his throat. He threw the shirt on the floor and pulled his jeans off, discarding them along with his underpants. She caught her breath as he turned back to her, magnificently naked.

Roughly he unzipped her shorts, and she lifted her hips to help him slide them off. ''I won't promise you children,'' he said. His lips found her navel above her bikini panties, his hand splayed on her stomach and then moved lower, nudging the satin down. His fingers touched, lightly explored, and she writhed at the exquisite pleasure of it.

She pulled down the strap of her bra, silently begging, and Jager took the hint, his lips brushing the curve of her breast even as his hand went to the clasp, freeing her from the garment.

"All I can give you," he said, as it followed their other clothing to the floor, "is myself. And this..."

Then his mouth closed over her breast and she was spinning in the ether. His hands wove magic and his mouth intoxicated, and within a blessedly short time he was plunging into her and she was rising to meet him in an ecstasy of mutual need and fulfillment, a kaleidoscope of sensations so deep and so explosive she thought she'd break into a million glittering pieces before it was over.

And even as she lay panting in the aftermath, he began again, his hands gliding over her, his seduction sweet and slow this time, but knowing, remembering what she liked and exactly how she liked it. Bringing back poignant memories of other times, other places.

Paige reciprocated, touching him in the old ways, adoring him with her fingers, her lips, her tongue. Enjoying the guttural male purr of satisfaction he gave when she stroked him and tasted the salt musk of his skin.

This lovemaking was less frenetic, but even more satisfying, and the earth-shattering climax that clutched at her after she spread herself along his body and eased onto him until she held him deep and firm inside was enough to banish from her mind any thoughts of what tomorrow might bring.

* * *

When it came, she woke to see Jager coming into the room, freshly showered and wearing only his jeans.

He finger-combed damp hair from his forehead, and his jewel eyes lit on her. "Are you all right?"

"Yes." Her voice was husky. She tried to sit up without letting the sheet fall from her naked breasts, that still tingled from last night's ministrations. She lifted a hand to push fine hair out of her eyes and the sheet slipped.

Jager's eyes shifted, and she made a conscious effort not to coyly hitch the linen back into place. He swooped to pick up his shirt and shrug into it. "I've got to go," he said. "I have an early appointment, and I need to get home and change first." Already she could see him assuming his business persona, his expression becoming purposeful, remote, an intriguing and slightly unsettling transformation.

He glanced at his expensive watch. "I'll come back tonight, if that's okay." But he didn't sound as though he expected any argument. He sat on the bed to pull on his sneakers, then turned and brushed his lips across hers. For just an instant his eyes searched her face. "See you then," he said and left her. Seconds later she heard the slam of the front door.

Paige spent the day in a kind of daze. She must have got up and gone to work, because she found herself there, going through the motions of doing her job, apparently functioning normally. But she was on autopilot.

Until she'd driven home and desultorily tidied scraps of wallpaper and last night's dishes, and then Jager arrived, bringing a box of Chinese takeaways and a bottle of white wine. And suddenly she was alive again, every nerve end humming with anticipation and excitement.

He dished up the food, poured the wine and even produced a candle from a package he'd brought with him. A short, squat gold candle in a bubble-filled Venetian glass holder.

She remembered when they'd been just newly married he'd splashed out on fish and chips one night, produced a stub of a candle from somewhere and waxed it to a saucer disguised with leaves from a miserable, struggling grapevine in the neglected yard.

Blinking away tears of nostalgia, Paige took a sip of wine and spooned fragrant rice onto her plate, hardly making a dent in the feast spread before her. Jager had bought all her favorite Chinese dishes, things they'd scarcely ever been able to afford on their meager budget, and certainly not all at once. "We'll never eat all this!" she said.

"Give it a go," he answered, spearing a sweet-and-sour shrimp. "Anything we don't finish will keep."

They drank all the wine, and he toasted her with the last of it, his eyes full of promises. Promises of sweetness, of ecstasy, of physical fulfillment—and nothing more.

She couldn't complain that he hadn't warned her. Last night he'd been brutally frank about his intentions, and she hadn't made a murmur of protest.

And now it was too late to undo what they'd done. And what point was there in denying herself what Jager was willing to give? More than just sex, whatever he said.

He could withhold commitment, and even love. He could refuse to let her into his mind, and lock her out of his heart. But when he was in her arms and his body had become a part of hers, he couldn't wholly command his physical need for her, nor hide his emotions.

He might have had a much less complicated sexual relationship with any number of women—and very likely had, in the years they'd been apart. Paige bit her tongue on the unreasoning jealousy aroused at the thought. But he'd pursued her from the moment they met again. Despite her less than spectacular looks, despite the bitter failure of their marriage, and all the years between then and now, something had drawn him back to her.

All I can give you is myself...and this.

She'd settle for that. At least for a while. Lifting her glass, she returned the toast.

After the meal Jager made her stay in her chair while he cleaned up the table. And then wiped his hands, came to her and kissed her with a new gentleness, before leading her along the darkened passageway to her bedroom.

Paige was slipping into sleep when the bedroom phone rang. She had to get out of bed to find it because the room was still at sixes and sevens, but she crawled back under the sheets with the receiver in her hand. Jager turned and draped an arm over her midriff.

"Paige?" Maddie's voice queried. "You weren't asleep, were you?"

"No. Hi, how was the wedding?"

"Lovely, great fun. How's the decorating going?"

"Finished, really. All the wallpaper's hung."

"Finished?" Maddie's voice became muffled as she relayed the news to Glen in the background. "Did Jager help?"

"Yes, he's been…very useful." She smiled as Jager's lips nibbled her shoulder.

"Paige—I sort of let slip to Mother and Dad last week that he was…you know, helping out at the cottage."

So that was why their mother had been so anxious to introduce her to Philip. She couldn't help a small laugh. If anything, the plan had catapulted her into Jager's arms. One look at a potential rival and all his male territorial instincts had come to the fore. Within thirty-six hours he'd been in her bed.

He was in her bed now, feathering tiny kisses down her spine, his hand resting possessively on her hip.

Maddie said, "It's all right, then? You don't mind?"

"It's not a secret."

Jager sat up, raising his brows at her. "What?" he mouthed.

Paige shook her head. Maddie was saying, "I think they were wrong about him, anyway. I was too young at the time to have an opinion, and I hardly ever saw him, but I thought he was great-looking."

"He…he was," Paige agreed. His mouth was playing havoc with her, wandering in places that made her blood run hot.

"Mum and Dad can't say now that he's a no-hoper, can they? I mean, look at him!"

Paige was looking at him. He looked wonderful, all toned muscle and tanned skin. "No, they can't. Um, Maddie, I'm a bit tired…all that renovating…I need an early night."

After she'd switched off and put down the phone Jager said, "Tired?"

"Lazy." She slid down in the bed without dislodging the hand that had settled on her breast. "Oh, that's so good. Don't stop now."

"Maddie?" He sounded lazy too, but he didn't stop, his clever fingers making her skin tingle pleasurably. "What was that about?"

"You, mostly. She thinks you're terrific."

"I'm flattered. What about you?"

"Me?" She thought he was a superb lover and a complex human being, possibly a damaged one. And she suspected his motives.

Maybe her attraction for him was based on the fact that he'd once been considered not good enough to marry her. And maybe his determination to make her his mistress—implicit in the terms he'd spelled out—was a way to get back at all of them for past humiliation. "I think you don't need me to flatter your ego," she said, wondering if that was true. But if he needed her for anything but a bedmate, she knew he would be dragged by wild horses rather than admit it.

Philip phoned the following evening, while Paige and Jager were sharing her couch and listening to a CD he'd bought that day. She lay across his lap, her head

cradled by his shoulder. If she closed her eyes she
could imagine the years had fallen away and they
were teenagers again, newly wed and still giddy with
the novelty of being married.

The telephone bell shattered the mood, and she
struggled up to go into the hallway and answer.

To hide her reluctance she greeted Philip warmly,
and after telling him the job was finished thanked him
again for his help and repeated her invitation. "When
will you be having the children again? Sunday afternoon, then. Anytime. Yes, of course the dinner invitation stands. I'll look forward to it."

When she reentered the sitting room the music was
over and Jager was taking the disk out of the machine.
He closed the plastic case with a snap and put it aside.
"Philip?"

"Yes." She went back to the sofa and sat down.
"I invited him—"

"I heard."

Her eyes met his defiantly. "I'd promised. I can't
go back on my word."

The silent lift of his brows and the sardonic curl of
his mouth reminded her as surely as if he'd accused
her that she had once gone back on her solemn marriage vows. Unconsciously her hands clenched
against the fabric of the sofa.

Jager's voice was deceptively mild. "Do you hear
me arguing?"

Loud and clear. But not in words. Resisting the
urge to excuse or apologize, she said, "It wouldn't
make any difference if you did." She wished he
would come back to the sofa and pull her into his

arms again instead of standing over her with that slightly forbidding expression.

"You realize you're giving him a misleading message?"

"I haven't given him any message at all," Paige snapped, "except one that says I appreciated his help. And I won't be." She would ensure Philip knew that any romantic involvement was out of the question.

"Thank you."

"It has nothing to do with you." She wasn't going to let him think he could order her life, her friendships. He had offered her so little of himself. "I'm not pandering to your wishes, Jager, just because we're sleeping together. So don't expect it."

A lambent flame flickered in his eyes. "Spoiling for a fight, darling?"

"No." She didn't want to fight him. She wanted to make love with him—fierce, all-consuming, mind-numbing love. "I just want you to know you can't steamroller me. You can't take over my life."

"Have I ever steamrollered you?"

Paige bit her lip. "No," she admitted. Even last night he'd given her every chance to repulse him if she'd wanted to. He was formidably self-assured and sexually confident, but that didn't make him a bully. If she'd been overwhelmed by him that was down to her own susceptibility. The stark fact was she wanted him, at least as much as he wanted her.

He strolled over to her, the fitful gleam in his eyes intensifying. "I'm glad we cleared that up. Now—" he bent and took both her hands in his, drawing her to her feet "—shall we go to bed?"

*   *   *

Philip's children were a nice, well-behaved pair, and the afternoon went pleasantly. When dinner was over Philip helped Paige wash up while the children watched a video in the sitting room.

"Thanks for this," he said, hanging up the tea towel, then coming close. "It's been nice, Paige."

"I'm glad." She moved unobtrusively further from him. "Like I said, I owed you."

He leaned against the sink counter and regarded her thoughtfully. "Seen Jager lately?"

"Yes, actually. I'm seeing quite a lot of him."

His lips pursed ruefully. He nodded. "I missed out there, then?"

"You're a very nice man, Philip."

"Thank you." He inclined his head. "And you're a nice woman." He paused. "I get the feeling there's not a lot of softness in Jager. I wouldn't want to see you hurt."

She was touched. "I appreciate your concern, but I can handle Jager." Even as she said it, she wondered if it was true. She could get badly burned...again.

"Okay. I'll mind my own business." Philip stepped forward to kiss her cheek. "I hope it works out for you."

Jager phoned later, after Philip and the children had left.

"Are you checking up on me?" Paige demanded.

"Don't be so touchy. I called to say good night. I could come round if you like."

Tempted, Paige decided not to give in. Jager was like a drug to her—the more she had of him the more she craved him. "I'm tired," she said. "Children have so much energy."

For a moment she thought he'd gone. Then he said, "How's Philip?"

"He seems fine."

"You let him down gently?"

"Stop fishing, Jager," she said crisply. "Will I see you tomorrow?"

"Is that an invitation?"

"If you like."

"Then I'll be there. Unless you'd like to come to my place?"

"No." She could barely cope with him on her own territory. She wasn't sure how she felt about venturing into his.

He laughed. "Okay. I'll bring dinner."

It didn't take Maddie long to figure out that Paige and Jager were sleeping together. Jager certainly made no effort to hide it, and pride wouldn't allow Paige to suggest they keep it secret.

"Do the parents know?" Maddie asked her, agog.

"Not yet." They were bound to find out, Paige supposed, but she wasn't anxious to break the news.

"I won't tell," Maddie promised.

"It doesn't really matter anymore, Maddie."

"Do you think…you might get married again?"

"It's not in our plans."

They had no plans, they were living wholly in the present. From day to day she didn't know if Jager would be sharing her bed that night or not. If she was going to be out she let him know. He scrupulously never asked where or why.

He'd begun to leave a toothbrush, shaver and comb in her bathroom, clothes in her wardrobe. She kept a couple of cans of his favorite beer in the fridge.

When she shopped for floor rugs Jager accompanied her. He helped her hang curtains and choose where the pictures should go on the walls. At a flea market they found an antique oval mirror for the bedroom, where the bed was now in pride of place and Paige had arranged an Indian sari, gleaming in red silk with delicate gold edges, in a graceful swathe on the silk-look gold-papered wall behind it.

She'd spent an extravagant amount on a lush wine velvet bedspread honeycombed with gold thread, and tossed silk cushions in gold and shades of red and purple against the pillows, the colors echoing the Persian rug on the floor. Colors of passion.

She fell for an ebony figurine of an almost life-size sleek, crouching black leopard with gleaming green glass eyes, and placed it beside a red velvet footstool in a corner of the room. Then, deciding she might as well go all the way, she hung several gold chains around its neck. And on the dressing table she crowded a dozen brass candlesticks of varying sizes and designs, furnishing them with red or gold candles.

"It looks like a love-nest!" Maddie exclaimed when she saw the room next. "Fantastic!"

When everything was in place Jager looked around the room, his gaze lingering on the leopard for a few seconds, then he reached for Paige, drew her toward the bed and pressed her down among the cushions, kissing her with passion and purpose. Later he dispensed with the bedspread and most of the cushions, but made good use of those that were left.

The next evening he arrived with a large flat parcel, and she unwrapped it to find a gilt-framed reproduction of Ingres' *Odalisque with a Slave,* the naked Eastern beauty in her sumptuous surroundings reclining against cushions that exactly matched Paige's bedroom walls.

He had trumped her leopard.

"Are you having a housewarming?" Maddie asked her.

Paige hadn't thought about it, but it might be as good a way as any to introduce their parents to the idea of her and Jager being a couple again.

She invited Philip, and a few people from her work, and the neighbors. The little house was full to overflowing, the guests spilling onto the porch and even into the garden, although the nights were cool now.

Jager greeted Paige's parents courteously, accepted their stiff nods, and found a chair for her mother.

"I'll take your coat," Paige offered as Margaret doffed the jacket she was wearing. "And Jager will get you a drink."

When she returned from the bedroom Jager and Glen were fiddling with the stereo while her parents, drinks in hand, talked with Philip.

She was distracted by some more arrivals and it wasn't until much later that her mother cornered her on the excuse of needing the bathroom, claiming she had forgotten where it was.

"That young man seems very much at home," Margaret commented as they edged through the crowd.

Paige said firmly, "Jager? Yes, he is. He spends a lot of time here."

Her mother cast her a look. "Your father says he's hugely successful, but leopards don't change their spots, and after Aidan...well, I hope you know what you're doing."

"Yes, I know what I'm doing."

"I see Philip's here," Margaret said hopefully. "I thought you and he got on rather well."

"He helped with the decorating. Actually he and Jager get on rather well too." They reached the bathroom and Paige opened the door. "Here you are."

"Good party," Jager said afterward, as they lay entwined in her bed. The leopard's glass eyes gleamed in the moonlight spilling into the room between filmy swathed curtains. A big moth flung itself against the window and blundered off into the night.

"I think so." Paige yawned.

His voice dry, he asked, "Do you think your parents got the message?"

She hadn't discussed that aspect with him at all. But he wasn't stupid. "They know we're...together."

"And...?"

"And what? I love my parents but they don't decide how I should run my life."

"How do they feel about it now that I'm not exactly on the poverty line?"

"Money had nothing to do with it. If we'd been older—"

"Do you really think that would have made much difference?"

She would never convince him. He had a blind spot as far as her parents were concerned, just as they did about him. "It's all in the past anyway. Can't we talk about something else?"

"Better still," he said, "let's not talk at all."

His mouth came down on hers, and within minutes she was incapable of talking, even of thinking, her whole being concentrated on the wonderful sensations he was creating, and the need to make him feel the same.

CHAPTER NINE

JAGER asked Paige to hostess a dinner party for him. "I'll get caterers in," he said, "but I'd like you to be there. By my side."

She hadn't ever set foot in his home. After the first couple of times when she'd evaded the suggestion, he had stopped asking. They went together to the theater or dinner or sporting events where they mixed with the sort of people her parents knew. Once they even attended the same social function as her mother and father and engaged in a short, formal chat. But wherever they went, afterward he returned her to the cottage and more often than not stayed the night.

She hadn't been wrong about the kind of relationship he'd offered her. She saw the satisfaction in his eyes when she dressed up, choosing clothes that without crossing the bounds of good taste instilled by her mother, emphasized her figure, distracting attention from her face. Dresses that hugged or flowed, were cut low in front or back; slit skirts, short skirts—though not too short; and for casual occasions, jeans that molded her neat bottom and hugged her long legs.

"This is Paige Camden," Jager would introduce her, his possessive arm encircling her waist, the pride in his eyes as they slipped over her proclaiming she was his. And more often than not, the other person said interestedly, "Oh...Henry's daughter?"

And she'd feel Jager's fingers on her waist as she acknowledged her parentage.

She was Jager's trophy, but no longer his wife.

"What sort of dinner party?" she inquired cautiously. They were dining at one of the exclusive—and expensive—restaurants he preferred. She picked up her wine from the impeccable linen tablecloth and sipped it to hide her trepidation.

"I owe some hospitality to a few people. You remember the Zimmermans? And the Hardys."

They had been guests of both couples. Married couples. She pushed the thought aside. "Anyone else?"

He shrugged. "I thought about ten people."

"It's quite a large party for dinner."

"I have a big dining table. The apartment is planned for entertaining."

She knew it was a serviced apartment in the central business district, a gracious old building converted at great cost to meet the demands of people like Jager who had the money to pay for service and style and preferred living near their city offices.

Paige put down the wineglass, watching the red liquid settle back into stillness, the light gleaming on it.

"And maybe Maddie and Glen," Jager persuaded. "We've eaten with them often enough."

They had, although sometimes her sister and brother-in-law dropped in at the cottage and stayed for an impromptu meal.

She looked up and found him regarding her intently. There was a tenseness about his shoulders, a tightening around his mouth. She saw this was important to him.

Paige had never analyzed her own reluctance to take this further step in their relationship. It was common knowledge now that they were lovers. They had appeared together in public often enough, and invitations frequently included them both. Even the Zimmermans, both in their sixties, had assigned them a double bedroom during a weekend visit to the couple's beach house.

"When do you plan to have this dinner party?" she asked. "And how formal will it be?"

Jager didn't smile but she sensed the easing of tension in him. He knew he'd won.

A few evenings later he arrived at the cottage with a plastic carrybag bearing the logo of a designer boutique. "I brought you a present," he said. "I hope it fits."

She opened the bag and took the carefully folded garment from its tissue wrapping, holding it by a pair of thin gold straps that cleverly curved around the front and turned into crisscrossed ties across a deep opening in the ruched black chiffon stretch bodice, and extended to an even lower one at the back. The bodice was thigh-length, and below that several soft layers of chiffon, each subtly edged with gold, flared into a short skirt.

It was beautiful and expensive and wildly sexy.

"I want you to wear it to my dinner party," Jager said. "Try it on."

Her fingers trembled. A small moth seemed to be fluttering in her throat. She let the dress drop back into the nest of tissue on the couch. "No," she said.

A frown appeared between his brows. "You don't like it? Black suits you. Believe me, you'll look great in that."

Paige knew she would. His instinct was unerring. In that dress she could be certain no one would be looking at her face.

She would look like his mistress.

Her hands tightened into fists. "I won't let you buy clothes for me, Jager."

The frown deepened. "I've bought you things before."

He'd bought lingerie for her, sexy undies and nightwear that she knew was as much for his pleasure as hers, but that she enjoyed wearing for him...in private. "This is different." The moth in her throat had turned into a hard, choking lump of ice.

"It's a dress," he said, impatiently, glancing at it. "What's so different about it? It's no more revealing than that green thing with the slit up to your thigh and the other slit in the front that drives me wild. Or that skimpy little black velvet top with the one button in front."

How could she explain her rejection of the concept of wearing a dress he'd chosen and paid for and asked her to wear? Her gut-level conviction that it would alter the carefully balanced status quo between them was unreasonable.

Intellectually she knew it didn't change anything. But somehow accepting his "gift" was accepting that she was no more to him than a sexual partner and a status symbol.

"It's...public," she said. "You want to show me off."

"It's a private dinner party," he argued. "I like showing you off. Any man would. Is that a crime?"

Paige gave up trying to make him understand. "I don't need another dress."

He looked thoughtful. "You haven't worn anything new lately."

That was true. She had spent most of Aidan's insurance money on the cottage and its refurbishment, keeping aside a small emergency fund. Her income was adequate and in time her father would leave her some money, but meantime she preferred to be independent, spending sensibly and cautiously. "I'm sorry if my wardrobe doesn't match up to your image," she said.

"When we were married one of your chief complaints was not having new things to wear."

She wished he hadn't reminded her. Unlike Jager, she'd never been able to bring herself to wear secondhand clothes. No doubt she'd been spoiled, as he'd scornfully told her.

Remembering how long he'd hung around outside the charity shop before entering, Paige had flung that at him, and he'd admitted that pride had warred with need. "But it's not so bad. And you were great. I watched how you handled the customers, friendly but respectful, just as if you were serving in some Queen Street store. That was class.''

In the face of his patent admiration, the quarrel died then, and she'd even swallowed her misgivings and tried buying used clothes, but her revulsion at wearing something that had belonged to someone else—perhaps someone who had died—was uncontrollable.

This was a different emotion, but just as strong. ''If you want me to wear something new,'' she said, ''I'll buy it myself.''

''That isn't the point.''

''Then what is?''

He looked back at her in wordless anger. It seemed he was no more able to articulate his reasons than she was.

''Never mind,'' he said finally. ''If you don't want it…'' He shrugged, obviously baffled.

She'd spoiled his surprise, spurned his gift. And if she suspected his motives, she supposed they were subconscious and he was genuinely puzzled by her refusal. ''I'm sure they'll take it back,'' she said, bending to replace the wrappings.

''I won't be taking it back,'' Jager said harshly. ''Keep it, in case you change your mind. Or give it away.''

She wouldn't be changing her mind, but perhaps forcing him to take it back would exacerbate any hurt he was feeling. Not that he showed hurt—only a tight-lipped frustration. She slipped the rewrapped dress into the bag. ''How are the dinner plans going? Did you ask Glen if he and Maddie could come?''

''They're coming.'' The anger hadn't quite died

but his voice was neutral. "I haven't finalized yet with a couple of people. We'll probably be twelve in all."

Paige did buy a new dress. It wasn't as sexy nor as costly as the one that now sat at the back of a high shelf in her wardrobe, still in its bag. But it was soft and pretty, sage-green with a wide though modest neckline. And if Jager was disappointed when he opened the door to her after a whisper-quiet, mirrored elevator whisked her to his penthouse apartment, he didn't show it by a flicker of an eyelid.

He ushered her into a large, high-ceilinged room. A wall of windows looked out on the harbor, inky-black by night except where lights shimmered in snaking lines from anchored ships, the high arch of the Harbor Bridge, and shoreside buildings.

With a view like that the designer had wisely not tried to compete. The furniture was plain and almost stark, long couches covered in palest gray leather, occasional tables carved of light wood, with glass tops. Paige's high heels sank into unobtrusively gray-green carpet, and color was added by strategically placed rugs and large paintings.

A wide archway revealed the dining table, already set with gleaming cutlery and wineglasses.

She had arrived early, mindful of her hostess duties. "I see the table's fixed."

"The caterers did that first. They're in the kitchen now—come and meet them."

A pleasant middle-aged couple, the caterers seemed to have everything under control. Within minutes

Paige was back in the living room while Jager poured her a drink.

She couldn't help mentally comparing their surroundings to the cramped quarters they'd shared over ten years before. It was difficult to believe Jager was the same person.

They had both changed since then. He'd been the one who insisted on marriage, on commitment, a blind leap of faith in the future—their future. Security and permanence. Now she understood that he'd never had that from anyone, but at seventeen she hadn't comprehended how desperately he needed it from her. Under the surface brashness and stubbornness had been a deep-seated craving she'd been too young to understand, too inexperienced to fulfill.

Apparently he had found what he wanted in his career and his hard-earned wealth. This Jager no longer needed validation nor moral support from her. He didn't want her promises or her love. It was enough that he had access to her body, her company when he felt so inclined, her presence at his side when a presentable social partner was required.

"What's the matter?" Jager asked. Glass in hand, he was lounging on a sofa opposite her, and in the big room seemed distant, both physically and emotionally.

"Nothing." He must have read in her face the aching tug of regret for what might have been. She looked around them. "This is…impressive."

"More so than your parents' house?"

Theirs was large and architect-designed, with a pool and garden where Paige and Maddie had spent happy hours with their friends when they were growing up. It was a family home, the decor chosen by their mother with comfort as well as entertaining in mind achieving a balance of elegance and welcome.

"Do you need to compare?" she challenged him.

His gaze was enigmatic. "It's just an idle question."

Jager never asked idle questions, but she didn't want to start a fight before his guests arrived. She took some of her drink and changed the subject, commenting on the view.

When the doorbell chimed she was relieved. More people would dissipate the subtle tension in the air.

The Zimmermans had barely settled with their drinks when Maddie and Glen breezed in, holding hands. Every time their eyes met they smiled as though they simply couldn't help it. Marriage seemed to have made their feelings for each other even stronger, and Paige felt a pang of pure envy.

While Jager was handing Maddie a glass the doorbell sounded again and he went to answer it.

Paige was talking to Maddie on one of the sofas when he ushered in the new arrivals. Turning expectantly, she suffered a jolt when she saw her parents enter the room, restrained social smiles fixed on their faces.

White wine spilled over her hand as she stood up. Carefully she put down the glass and picked up a paper napkin to wipe it away. "You didn't tell me!" she accused Jager.

"I thought I'd surprise you."

Her mother wafted over and kissed her. "Aren't you pleased to see us?"

"Yes, of course." She returned the kiss and forced a smile for her father as he saluted her cheek too.

She looked at Jager, trying to divine why he'd done this, but he was asking Margaret what she wanted to drink, and then as the doorbell chimed yet again he asked Paige, "Would you pour a dry white for your mother, darling, while I get that?"

There was no chance to speak with him privately. At dinner she took her place opposite Jager and played the part he'd assigned her, keeping the conversations going, discreetly signaling to the caterers when the next course should be served, and making sure everyone was well fed and comfortable.

Afterward they had coffee and liqueurs. The caterers cleaned up and left, and while Paige talked with the Zimmermans she saw Jager approach her father, who was admiring the view from the window.

Henry turned, a little grim and wary, and she couldn't see Jager's expression, but she noted the way he inclined his head with a hint of respect for the older man.

That was a new tactic. When she'd first introduced them, after one of the women at the charity shop dropped a hint to her mother that she'd been "seeing some boy" and Margaret had suggested she bring her new friend to meet her parents, there had been no hint of deference in Jager.

He'd eyed the marble-floored foyer and graceful staircase with studied indifference, and when she ushered him into the comfortably though expensively furnished sitting room to meet her parents, his fast but comprehensive survey of the room seemed slightly disparaging.

He'd looked Henry squarely in the eye and called him ''sir'' but a note of irony in his voice made Henry glance at him sharply and Paige's nails dig into her palms. Her mother's careful smile of welcome elicited no more than a nod and a casual "Hi," as he took her outstretched hand.

He'd answered her mother's delicate questions about his background almost truculently, as if daring her to find fault with his lack of antecedents or education. And he seemed to go out of his way to emphasize the differences between his lifestyle and theirs. It hadn't been a comfortable visit, and Paige had braced herself for criticism later.

It had been veiled in slightly pained surprise that she could be attracted to ''that type of boy'' and patronizing pity at his upbringing and poor career prospects. But they hadn't really taken the relationship seriously until the bombshell of her marriage. After that her parents and Jager had become implacable enemies.

They didn't look like enemies now. Henry actually clapped Jager's shoulder as they left, and Margaret said with rather astonished sincerity, ''We've had a very nice evening, Jager. I did enjoy talking with Serena Zimmerman.''

Maddie and Glen were the last to leave, lingering when the other guests had gone.

They sat side by side on one of the sofas, Maddie snuggled into her husband's encircling arm. As soon as Jager returned to the room Maddie said, "Sit down, Jager. We have something to tell you two!"

Looking at her sister's radiant face, Paige guessed before Maddie blurted out, "We're pregnant!"

Ashamed of the split second of sheer jealousy that attacked her without warning, Paige jumped up to embrace her. "Congratulations, I can see you're thrilled. Do Mother and Dad know? They didn't say anything tonight."

"I phoned Mum yesterday when the test confirmed it, but she knew I wanted to tell you myself."

Jager rose to shake Glen's hand and kiss Maddie's cheek. "This calls for another drink," he said.

But Maddie shook her head. "I'm not allowed." She'd asked for a soft drink when she arrived, Paige recalled, and left her wineglass at dinner virtually untouched.

Glen declined too, saying they'd better get home as Maddie tired easily.

Closing the door behind them, Jager turned to Paige. "You're going to be an aunt."

"And you'll be an uncle."

Seemingly the thought hadn't occurred to him. A surprised smile curled his mouth. "I suppose so."

"Why didn't you tell me you'd invited my parents?" she demanded.

He looked slightly taken aback at the aggression in her tone, steering her back into the living room. "I wasn't sure they'd actually turn up. I didn't want you to be disappointed."

"Why did you ask them?"

"I thought you'd be pleased."

Or he'd wanted to flaunt her, their daughter, in their faces. She recalled the dress he'd bought—a statement if ever there was one. Inside her there was a hollow feeling. "How did you persuade them?"

A cynical curve to his mouth, he said, "I'm not beneath their standards of acceptability anymore. A few million dollars makes a difference."

"Why won't you believe me?" she snapped. "Money wasn't the issue."

He stopped in the middle of the room, and pulled her against him. "Let's not argue," he said huskily, his lips nuzzling her temple. He lifted a hand and turned her face up to him. "You were a wonderful hostess. Thank you."

For a thank-you kiss it was pretty devastating. He parted her lips and took full advantage of her compliance. As always, his kisses and the strength of his arms, the tender, arousing stroking of his hands, heated her body and quickened her breath, but this time her mind wouldn't be stilled.

She broke away, and he let her go. His mouth looked full and softer than usual, his eyes glittering, glazed. "You didn't bring a bag," he said.

"I'm not staying."

"You know I want you to."

"No. I haven't anything with me."

"I keep spare toothbrushes, and there's a heated towel rail in the bathroom. You can wash your undies and they'll dry before morning."

"I'm tired." And then she despised herself for making excuses.

"You can sleep here. If sleep is what you want."

When she made to object again he reached out and put his fingers over her mouth. "For some reason you're mad at me. I don't want you going away angry, Paige. We don't need to make love if you'd rather not. Just share my bed."

She *was* angry, in a confused, hurt way. Angry at herself as much as at him. And not quite sure why.

Part of it was because of what she saw as his one-upmanship over her parents and his determined refusal to see their point of view.

But part of it too was Maddie and Glen's announcement. Their delight in starting a family, that ultimate proof of a belief in a lasting bond between them, cruelly highlighted the nature of Jager and Paige's relationship. No promises, no ties except the ephemeral, easily broken one of sexual compatibility.

It wasn't enough.

The nagging little ache hadn't gone away. It was growing, filling her whole chest. Her eyes stung, and she put a hand up and bent her head into it to hide the incipient tears. The last thing she wanted was to cry in front of Jager.

"You *are* tired," he said. He lifted her into his arms, cradling her like a child. She squeezed her eyes shut while he carried into the hallway and through to the darkened master bedroom. Anger came to the fore again, stemming the tears. "Jager, I told you—"

"Shh." He lowered her to the bed, and when she tried to struggle up, held her wrists. "Rest. I'll sleep in the spare room if you like. I'm not asking anything of you, Paige, just giving you a bed for the night.

Now sit up and I'll unzip you and hang up that dress. It's too pretty to sleep in.''

It made any further insistence seem totally unreasonable. With a strong suspicion that his determination to have her stay was as irrational as her own reluctance to do so, she gave in. This pointless fight was only a symptom of much deeper issues at the heart of their relationship. Maybe the time had come to confront them. But not tonight.

She sighed, let him help her to sit up and bent forward for him to pull down the zip.

''I'll wash out your undies for you if you like,'' he offered.

Something caught in her throat. Stupid to be affected by that—a simple, practical but so intimate an action. She shook her head. ''I'll change them when I get home tomorrow.'' She slid her feet under the cover as he pulled it aside for her, and took off her glasses to place them on the bedside table.

Jager was hanging up her dress. ''Do you need the bathroom?'' he asked her.

''No.'' She'd used it about an hour ago, and cleaned her teeth too. She always carried a toothbrush. For once her makeup could stay on overnight. ''You don't need to sleep in the spare room,'' she said to his back, and saw him pause, his shoulders rigid, before he closed the wardrobe door. ''But I do mean to sleep.''

He kissed her nose. ''I won't be long.''

Although the bed was big enough for them to sleep comfortably without touching, Paige was glad when he slipped in beside her and she felt his body warm against her back, his arms around her. His breath feathered her nape in what sounded like a sigh of content.

Paige closed her eyes against the confusing mixture of emotions that threatened to overwhelm her, fighting tears. Fighting the growing conviction that they couldn't go on like this—*she* couldn't go on like this. And that this might be the last time they shared a bed.

She must have slipped into sleep quite quickly, despite the turmoil in her mind. When she woke she was alone. A black satin kimono lay at the end of the bed.

She took the kimono and went into the bathroom. Fifteen minutes later she had showered, and dried her newly washed panties with the hair dryer fixed to the wall, wondering if Jager ever used it, or if it was strictly for female visitors. But then, it was probably just one of the extra touches of luxury the designers had provided in all the apartments.

The dress she'd worn last night hardly seemed suitable for breakfast. She stepped into the panties and belted the roomy robe over them before going down the passageway.

The aroma of frying bacon met her. Besides the table in the center of the dining area, a small oval table and two chairs were set near the window. Last night it had served as a sideboard, but now it was laid for breakfast.

She entered the kitchen and Jager turned from putting bread into the toaster. "Just in time," he said, depressing the lever. "I heard you in the shower. If you want fruit, there are tinned peaches."

"Just juice, thanks." There were already glasses of it on the table.

. He pulled the lid off a covered pan and slid crisp bacon and perfectly cooked eggs onto two plates, then added a slice of toast to each.

A plate in each hand, he came toward her, bent to press a kiss on her mouth and said, "You look great in my robe. Sexy. Come and eat."

CHAPTER TEN

PAIGE wasn't really hungry, but eating gave her an excuse to delay the inevitable. Even to consider the cowardly alternative of leaving things as they were, of accepting whatever crumbs of his life Jager was willing to share with her for as long as it suited him.

A bleak thought.

"You slept well," Jager commented, buttering his toast. "I was tempted to wake you, but you looked so peaceful I controlled myself."

"You want a medal?" she asked sardonically. Half of her wished he'd followed his instinct, made love to her one more time, while the other half told her it would only have made this even harder, maybe impossible.

"No medal, but I wouldn't turn down a reward."

His gaze slid over her and she looked away. Flirting wasn't on the menu this morning, and as for anything else... She concentrated on cutting into her bacon.

Later Jager took her plate away and made coffee. "You're very thoughtful," he said, placing her cup before her and resuming his seat.

Paige stirred sugar into her cup, taking her time. "I think we should talk."

"About what?"

She looked up at the wary expression on his face,

the slight frown. "About our relationship. About... what we want from each other."

Jager leaned back, his eyelids drooping so that his black lashes veiled his eyes. "What do you want?"

Paige replaced the spoon carefully in the saucer, glanced out at the view—the harbor in the morning light glittered blue and green, and yachts danced like white-winged birds on the waves.

Her hand crushed the silk of his borrowed robe in her lap. "I want things you can't give me," she said. *Or won't.* "I'm not blaming you, Jager. You didn't hold out any false hopes. But I'm—" she swallowed, because her heart was crying out against this "—I'm not willing to carry on with our...affair."

"Affair?"

"That's what it's called, Jager, when two people are sleeping together without commitment, without promises, free to break it off at anytime."

His face had gone oddly blank, his eyes lifeless. "Is that what you're doing? Breaking it off?"

She swallowed. "If it isn't...going anywhere, yes."

After a long moment he pushed back his chair and stood up. "You'd better get dressed," he said. "I'll take you home."

For a second or two she was stunned. That was it? No discussion, no protest, no attempt at persuasion, or even anger? Simply an acceptance that it was over? As if it didn't even *matter*.

She stared at the steaming, untouched coffee in front of her, stretched out a hand to pick up the cup, then realized her fingers were trembling, and let it clatter back into the saucer. A flash of sheer outrage took her to her feet, her shoulders stiff and straight. "I'll get a taxi," she said. She'd used one to come here, mindful of the fact that there would be drinks at dinner.

He didn't answer, but when she returned, dressed and with her head held high, he was standing in the doorway, his car keys in his hand. She didn't argue any further.

Neither of them spoke in the car. The ache in Paige's chest and throat was almost choking her. A tearing regret added itself to the ache. Why couldn't she have kept her mouth shut? Maybe with more time Jager would have…

He would have what? her mind jeered. Changed his mind? Decided to marry her after all? Vowed eternal love and devotion?

She reminded herself smartingly that fairy tales seldom happened in real life. She'd had her chance once with Jager and she'd blown it, bailed out when the going got rough. He wasn't going to forgive her for that, ever.

When he pulled up outside the cottage, she said, huskily, "Thank you," and gathered her bag and wrap with clumsy fingers.

"I'm coming in," Jager said.

Her heart gave a leap of hope, before she quelled it with stern reason. He probably just wanted to collect his things. "I'll send your stuff to you." She couldn't bear to watch him strip the cottage of every remnant of his frequent presence, every reminder of their time together.

"I'm coming in," he repeated, with a controlled ferocity that made her look at him, and what she saw stopped her heart. His face was white, pinched, and a tiny muscle throbbed near his jaw. He was quietly furious.

Curiously, she was more heartened than afraid. At least anger was an emotional reaction. It was his apparent indifference that had stunned her.

She led the way down the path and opened the door. "I want to change my clothes," she said. "I won't be long." Making it clear that she expected him to wait in the sitting room.

She stripped and pulled on fresh undies, jeans and a shirt. Then she took down the bag containing the dress Jager had bought. That strengthened her resolve. Two of his shirts hung in the wardrobe. She stuffed them in with the dress, followed them with a pair of trousers, a couple of pairs of socks, underpants. The bag was bulging.

In the bathroom she collected his shaving things, his toothbrush, and shoved them into a smaller bag, then lugged the lot into the sitting room.

"Here," she said, dumping the bags onto the couch. "You'd better take your CDs too."

He'd been standing at the window, looking out at the kowhai tree and the street beyond the hedge. He turned and looked at the bags as if he hadn't a clue what was in them. Comprehension dawned and slowly his gaze rose to her face. "There's no need for that."

"Isn't it what you came in for?"

Impatience creased his brow and darkened his eyes. "What the hell do I care about a few stupid clothes?"

Nothing, of course. What had once been a matter of vital importance was mere trivia to him now. "Then why insist on coming in?"

"To tell you that you've won," he said. "I can give you anything money can buy, Paige. I've given you myself—the new improved version that won't embarrass you before your family and friends. I've learned how to behave in the best company—even your parents must know that by now. But you want commitment, promises...? All right, you've got them. If that's what it takes to keep you."

Paige's head whirled at the unexpected, stunning turnabout. It should have made her happy. Instead she was filled with sick dismay. He didn't look as though he was making a declaration of love. More like a declaration of war. His voice was harsh, his eyes glittering with something akin to hostility. He paused, and then said, "So, my darling ex-wife...will you marry me...again?"

It shouldn't be like this, she thought. She should be in his arms, not facing him across the room as though they were enemies instead of lovers. He should be looking at her with tenderness, not that inimical, unrelenting green stare. Everything about the scene was wrong. This was far from a romantic dream coming true. It was a nightmare.

"No," she said. Self-preservation told her there was no other answer, although she could feel her heart splintering.

You've won, he'd said, but she hadn't won. If he

thought this was a battle, they were both losers. The latter part of their impetuous marriage, founded on love and ideals, had been bad enough. A second one, given Jager's clear resentment, his conviction that she'd forced him into a proposal, promised only another disaster.

"No?" He looked as if he'd been hit—hard.

She laughed—unsteadily, on the edge of crying. There was a kind of bitter humor in the situation. He was offering her exactly what she longed for, but in such a way that she'd be crazy to accept it. "No," she reiterated.

"What the hell kind of game are you playing now?" he demanded. "Ah—" he snapped his fingers "—I suppose you want your pound of flesh...my heart. All right, I love you! I admit it, freely. I loved you from the moment I set eyes on you, buzzing about that shop all earnest and purposeful and caring, and so damned efficient. I loved the purity of your profile when I first saw you serving at the counter— and when you looked at me through the window I loved the way your eyes were soft and misty and kind of vulnerable and yet wise behind those really serious glasses you wore. I've always loved you."

Paige didn't believe any of it. She folded her arms across herself as if she could ward off the barrage of his words, because he was throwing them at her like missiles rather than love-tokens.

"I'll love you till I die." Jager's eyes glowed like green fire. "Is that what you want to hear?"

She didn't, not if he didn't mean it. And everything in his tone suggested he didn't. Her throat felt raw.

Her whole body was shaking. "No," she managed to say again, scarcely more than a whisper. "Please go, Jager. Please."

A half-dozen expressions chased across his face. Rage, and chagrin, disbelief, briefly shock, and—surely not despair? For a moment he looked at her with piercing concern, until she stiffened her shoulders and met his gaze steadily, willing him to leave before she broke down.

He made an abrupt gesture, took a step toward her, but she quickly moved back and he stopped.

"All right," he said finally. "If that's what you want."

She didn't deny it, and after a few seconds he walked slowly past her and out of the front door.

Paige waited until she heard the car roar away before she collapsed onto the couch with a hand over her eyes, shivering despite the warmth of the sun streaming in the window, and trying to blot out thought, emotion, memory.

Her mother phoned later in the day to discuss Maddie's news. Margaret was ecstatic. Paige responded with as much enthusiasm as she could muster, but the events of the morning had left her feeling drained.

"And your father was quite impressed with Jager last night," Margaret said when she'd run out of comments on the prospect of a grandchild. "He says that young man has matured considerably."

"He *is* over thirty," Paige reminded her.

"Yes, well, apparently he has a good brain, Henry says."

"He always had a good brain." Paige couldn't seem to shake the habit of defending Jager.

"I suppose so," Margaret admitted. "But his manner left much to be desired. And I don't care what you say, you *were* too young to marry. He wasn't right for you then."

"I know, Mother," Paige agreed wearily.

"But...well, looking back, perhaps we might have helped a little. We did what we thought best at the time."

How ironic. Now, when it no longer made any difference, her parents were softening toward Jager. "It doesn't matter now."

Nothing mattered anymore.

She had to shake that feeling, Paige told herself in the following days. She got through them somehow, a matter of grim determination, getting out of bed, going through the motions of living and working, even eating regular meals, although nothing tasted as it should. It was like living in a thick, dreary fog; one that parted occasionally to give her glimpses of what real life was like, but she wasn't a participant.

She hadn't felt like this since the first few weeks after Aidan's death, nearly a year ago now. But she'd got over that, she realized with faint shock. Jager had helped her get over it.

And in some ways this was worse. Aidan was beyond human reach and nothing would bring him back. Jager was no more than a phone call away. She had only to dial his number and say one word—*yes*—to have him in her life again. But it would come with a cost. The cost of knowing that she'd backed him into a corner, made him feel emotionally blackmailed; and he might never get over his anger and resentment.

Relieved when the weekend came and she didn't need to drag herself to work and give an imitation of a living, breathing human being, she gave up trying to sleep in and tackled the garden instead. Already shrubs and perennials were flourishing, but weeds always threatened, and there was a warm, sheltered corner at the back of the house where she had decided to make a herb garden.

She was digging clods of earth and finding some satisfaction in chopping them with the sharp edge of the spade, when it was removed from her grasp and Jager said, "Here, let me do that."

Sheer happiness dizzied her for a golden moment before all the problems that beset them tumbled back into place. "I was doing all right," she said, wiping the back of a gloved hand over her damp forehead. Trust him to turn up when she was dirty and sweaty and in her oldest clothes, with not even her most minimal makeup on.

He glanced up, so briefly she had no time to see anything but the quick flash of his green eyes. "Sure," he said. "But I'll do it faster."

And with less effort, she acknowledged, watching the movement of his muscles under a white T-shirt and blue jeans. That's what he'd been wearing when she first saw him, but now the jeans had a designer label and the T-shirt wasn't threadbare.

Paige sat down on the back step and pulled off the gloves. Why was he here? She was afraid to ask.

He worked with an easy rhythm, and finished in half the time it would have taken her.

"Enough?" he queried her.

"Yes."

He lifted the spade and stuck it into the new garden bed, but stayed with his fingers curled around the handle, his eyes apparently studying the bare black earth. "I messed up the other night," he said. "Big time."

"Maybe we both did." Paige clasped her hands on her knees. "I didn't mean to make you feel trapped."

He looked up then but she had the feeling he wasn't really seeing her. "I suppose that's part of it."

"Part of it?"

"I was furious that you'd called my bluff." His eyes focused on her now. "I thought I'd got the upper hand, had you just where I wanted you."

Paige blinked. "You make it sound like a battle. What did you want, Jager, some kind of revenge?"

He altered his grip on the spade and looked down again, almost as though he planned to do more digging. "All I wanted was you. But I wanted—needed—to protect myself. I'd sworn I was never again going to descend to the hell you put me through when you left me, left our marriage. This time was going to be different. I was going to be in control. No vows, no promises to be broken. And if anybody dumped anybody, it was going to be me."

"I know you were holding back. You said you'd given me yourself, but you never really opened up to me." She asked with dull curiosity, "Did you plan to dump me?'' It would have been a just revenge, she supposed.

''I tried not to plan at all, after the first time we slept together here in your bed. Before that…well, it was different then.''

''Different, how?''

''It wasn't a coincidence, me being at your sister's wedding. After my father contacted me I had no particular reason to see him again. But on that first visit he told me about my brother and asked if I'd like to meet him. I let him talk, though I wasn't interested. Then he mentioned who Glen was marrying.'' He paused. ''Glen still thinks it was his own idea to invite me to the wedding.''

''You used him.''

''I used him to get invited here too.''

''Do you have *any* feelings for Glen, or your father?'' she demanded.

He seemed to think about it. ''Yes,'' he said finally. ''My father's a good man who made a stupid, drunken mistake when he was young and is doing his best to make up for it. I respect him for that. Glen…he's a friend. He's a good guy, honest and caring and dependable. There aren't too many like him. And his mother…'' With an air of surprise he said, frowning, ''I suppose I've grown fond of her. Finding out her husband had another child must have been hard, and she's handled it with dignity and generosity.''

''Were you using me too?''

His eyes darkened. ''Did it feel that way?''

''I felt more like a mistress than a lover,'' she said.

"I didn't think of it like that. All I knew was that I wanted you—had to have you."

"In your bed? Mine?" she corrected.

"In my life, Paige. And it seemed to be working. When I finally got you to come to my place I felt you'd moved a step closer. You were with me, you wanted me, and I hadn't had to expose my feelings at all, I was still able to pretend that my world wouldn't end if you left me again. There were no more promises of undying love to be flung back in my face."

"No commitment," Paige murmured.

"And then you whipped the rug from under my feet. It hadn't occurred to me—stupidly—that all you had to do was threaten to leave me to have me fold like a melting jelly. I suppose I never thought you'd do it. When you did, I felt...helpless."

"You?" She swept an ironic gaze over him, from the six-foot-plus top of his head over the arrogant nose and iron jaw, the rock-hard muscles of his chest and arms, and right down to his size twelve feet.

"I didn't like the feeling," he said. "I lashed out. I'm sorry."

Paige didn't know what to say. The silence grew, and Jager put a foot on the spade, then lifted it off again. He finally let go his grip on the handle and took a step toward her. "I'll promise anything," he said, "do anything, to have you back, Paige. If marriage is what you want, you have it. I didn't mean those things I said." He shook his head impatiently, then went down on his haunches in front of her, taking her hands in his. "Or I should say, I did mean them, but not the way I said them."

"You said you loved me," she reminded him, looking down at their joined hands.

"And that I always will. It's true. I can't help it, and I warn you that if you walk out on me again you won't get away so easily. I'll be doing my damndest to bring you back."

"You said you loved me the first time you saw me."

He rubbed his thumb over the back of one of her hands. "A slight exaggeration, maybe. I was attracted to you. I wasn't sure why, because you weren't my usual type."

"I wasn't pretty."

"Pretty!" He dismissed that with a scornful jerk of his head, as if the word were "trash" or "trivia." "You had more than prettiness. Elegance. Class. I liked that about you from the start."

"Inner beauty?" she inquired, resignedly. How often had her mother reminded her it was more important than being pretty to look at?

"No!" Jager said. "Yes, that too, I guess. But not only that." He gave her a puzzled look. "Paige...you surely don't think you're ugly?"

"Not ugly. Just plain."

"You're not plain!" He shifted his hands to her shoulders and gave her a little shake. "Not that it matters, but you are going to be a beautiful old lady when all the *pretty* girls have lost their looks. Yours is the kind of beauty that lasts, that gets better with age. I've told you often enough, you're lovely!"

"I thought you were just being…kind."

The shocked disbelief in his eyes convinced her. Jager really did think she was beautiful! And although she knew it wasn't really important, she couldn't help a thrill of delight. If Jager believed it, even if he were deluded, who cared what the rest of the world thought?

It was a liberating thought. For the first time she believed he meant it. And if he really did love her…

She said, "I don't want you to feel pressured into marriage. If you like we can go on just as we are." He had made some revelations today that helped her understand him much better than before, in fact he'd come right out and told her how he felt. Such a giant step, for the first time she could hope their relationship might become permanent. That this time they would make it.

He leaned over and kissed her lips, gently. "I need you, Paige, my first and only love, and I don't care what I have to do to make you need me."

"You don't have to do anything." Nothing he could do could make her need him any more than she did.

His eyes searched her face. "Glen asked me to be godfather to his baby," he said. "It made me think for the first time about what having a baby means."

The question had hardly arisen when they were married. They'd known they were too young, and financially they couldn't possibly have coped. "A baby?" Paige whispered.

"I never wanted to be a father before," Jager said. "Until I saw his—my father's—family, and then

Glen and Maddie, I didn't believe people who said love expands to new people. It had never happened to me. But with those two—you can see it growing daily. They're more in love than ever. It's... awesome.''

"You've been seeing them?'' Paige felt slightly guilty. She'd spoken to Maddie a couple of times on the phone but she hadn't wanted to see anyone, hugging her hurt and pain to herself on the excuse that she didn't want to cloud Maddie's happiness with her own misery.

"I needed to talk to Maddie about you. I figured she knew you better than anyone.''

"She never said.''

"Because I asked her not to. My pride had taken enough of a beating without you knowing I was begging your sister to tell me what to do to get you back.''

"What did she say?''

"She said, 'Be honest with her. And tell her you're sorry.' I'm being as honest as I can, Paige. And I'm asking you to forgive me. Can you?''

She loved him, and she was beginning to think that he truly loved her, despite her misgivings and his previous defensive attitude.

He'd been afraid of being hurt again. His mother had left him, then his aunt discarded him, and several foster homes had sent him away. All he'd known as a child was abandonment and betrayal. And when he thought he'd found his one true love and married her to prove that *he* was faithful and steadfast, she too had betrayed him, run away and repeated the cruel cycle.

"Can you forgive me?" she asked him. "For leaving you?" Because she knew he never had.

"You were barely more than a child," he said. "I asked too much of you. And your parents deliberately made it harder."

"My mother apologized for that, sort of, the other day."

He hesitated. "You always said they did it out of love."

"And you never believed that."

"It's an exclusive love," he said. "The kind that shuts out anyone who threatens what they want for you."

"Isn't that...?"

"Love of a kind," he conceded. "But did they care that they were hurting *you?* I won't do that to any child of mine. They wanted you to live the life they'd mapped out for you, not the one you wanted for yourself."

"I suppose," Paige acknowledged, "there's some truth in that. They could have been less...rigid. I hope I would be, that I'd support my children even when they made mistakes."

He stood up, taking her with him, so they stood face-to-face, as equals, even though he was taller. "Marry me again," he said quietly. "Bear my children, and love me all the days of my life, as I love you?"

It sounded like a solemn vow. She met his eyes. "If that's what you truly want."

"More than anything in the world. Ever since you left me I've been working toward this moment without knowing it. All my success, all the money I made, that fancy apartment I bought, was just to impress you."

"Oh, Jager!" she said, and almost apologetically, "I'm not impressed by that, you know."

Chagrin warred with his reluctant recognition of the truth. "I know," he confessed. "It doesn't mean anything to you, but it does to me."

"If it makes you happy," she said. "But if you lost it all tomorrow I'd still stick by you. Please believe that. I'm not seventeen and scared of real life anymore."

"I believe it, but it won't happen. I may not be as rich as Aidan, but—"

"Aidan wasn't rich!"

"Not by your father's standards, maybe—"

"Not by anyone's standards. He had a good job as an industrial chemist, but our home was mortgaged and...well, we weren't poor but we budgeted quite carefully. It was only with his insurance that I was able to buy this place."

He frowned down at her. "I assumed..."

"Wrong. But I suppose I can forgive you for that too. I've forgiven everything else."

"Everything?"

"Everything."

"So?"

She realized what he was waiting for. "Yes," she said. "I'll marry you."

He pulled her close and muttered into her hair,

"Thank you, darling, thank you!" Then he said, "It's a bit premature, but..."

And suddenly she was swung into his arms and carried through across the worn back doorstep, through the doorway and along the passageway to the bedroom.

"I'll miss this room," he said, depositing her on the bed and beginning to shuck his clothes.

"Miss it?" She watched him pull off the T-shirt, them, enjoying what he revealed.

"When we're married again." He unzipped his jeans and dropped them. Catching her inquiring look, he said, "You are going to live with me, aren't you?"

She sat up, and he perched on the bed and began to undress her too. Paige didn't stop him, lifting her arms to help him pull off her shirt, but said, "And give up the cottage?"

He undid her bra and tossed it aside. It landed on the leopard's ear and dangled. "I know you put a lot of work into it. *We* did."

"Then why can't we live here?"

Jager was looking rather greedily at her breasts, even as he unfastened her trousers and eased them down her legs. She didn't think he was listening. "Jager?" she insisted.

He pulled off the jeans and pushed her gently against the pillows, laying a hand on her breast as he kissed her, then lifted his head. "Don't you like the apartment? We can get another. Or a house. We'll need a house when the children arrive." He glanced down at what his hand was doing to her and smiled with satisfaction. "I'll find an architect—"

"Jager!" She gasped and wriggled, but held firm to her purpose. And his wrist. "I don't want to sell the cottage. Not yet anyway."

His hand finally stilled where it was. She said, "Why can't we live here?"

"Business," he said. "Entertaining. Besides..."

"Besides what?" she asked, and when he looked away, shrugging, she added fiercely, "Don't you dare clam up on me now! If I'm going to marry you I want to *know* what you're feeling."

"If?" he queried, his eyes narrowing.

"When we're married," Paige amended hastily, "and starting now! What is your problem?"

"I told you," he said unconvincingly. "But also—" he'd seen the threatening look on her face "—it was bought with your *other* husband's money."

"*My* money."

"From his insurance. It doesn't feel right."

"It seems to have felt perfectly all right until now."

"I didn't know then. And I haven't been living here. I can't," he said stubbornly. "Why do you think I've been trying to get you to my apartment since that first night?"

Exasperated, she said, "You can't be jealous of Aidan, Jager. He's dead."

"I'm not jealous." He scowled.

"Are you sure?" Paige reached up and smoothed back a strand of hair from the scowl. She hesitated, not wanting to denigrate Aidan, but decided to be honest. "I loved him, I won't pretend I didn't, but...it never felt the way it does with you."

The scowl lifted. "I've tried not to mind," he said. "I know I don't have any right."

She saw it had hurt him, but in time the hurt would ease. And she wouldn't let him ride roughshod over her. "I'm going to keep the cottage." She hoped he wasn't going to make it a bone of contention.

"You can. But I want our home to be *my* territory. Ours. Can you understand that?"

Yes, she could. He was sensitive about providing for her properly this time, showing her parents, with their old-fashioned values, that he could.

It might be a long while before he was utterly sure of her love, truly secure. She had a whole lifetime to prove it to him. Paige surrendered. "All right, I'll move into your apartment. But we could come here at weekends, maybe?"

"Done," he said promptly. "And I'll leave my cell phone behind. It'll be our secret hideaway, our love-nest in the suburbs."

She laughed softly. "Maddie said this room was like a love-nest."

"I'm glad I helped to create it," he said. "All that stripping and scraping away the years of covering up and neglect was worth it in the end." He looked around the room. "You've got rid of the accumulated rubbish and made it new and fresh again. Now—" he returned his attention to her, and lowered his mouth until it just touched her lips "—can we get on with what we're here for?"

He opened her mouth under his, and she arched into him, kissing him back without restraint, returning every caress, matching him in every way.

And when he gave her the ultimate physical delight and emotional fulfillment and she cried out against his mouth, and heard his answering groan, muffled in his throat, she knew that at last she had all of him, that he was wholly hers as she was wholly his. His wife again. Until the end of time.

The world's bestselling romance series.

HARLEQUIN®

Presents

Seduction and Passion Guaranteed!

Michelle Reid's
fantastic new trilogy

Hassan
Ethan
Rafiq
are

Hot-Blooded Husbands

Let them keep you warm tonight!

THE SHEIKH'S CHOSEN WIFE
#2254, on sale June

ETHAN'S TEMPTRESS BRIDE
#2272, on sale September

And look out for Rafiq's story,
on sale December

Pick up a Harlequin Presents® novel and you will
enter a world of spine-tingling passion and
provocative, tantalizing romance!
Available wherever Harlequin books are sold.

HARLEQUIN®
Makes any time special®

If you enjoyed what you just read,
then we've got an offer you can't resist!

Take 2 bestselling
love stories FREE!
Plus get a FREE surprise gift!

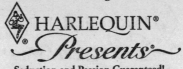

The world's bestselling romance series.

HARLEQUIN®
Presents

Seduction and Passion Guaranteed!

GREEK TYCOONS

They're the men who have everything—except a bride...

Wealth, power, charm—what else could a heart-stoppingly handsome tycoon need? In the GREEK TYCOONS miniseries you have already been introduced to some gorgeous Greek multimillionaires who are in need of wives.

Now it's the turn of favorite Presents author

Helen Brooks,

with her attention-grabbing romance

THE GREEK TYCOON'S BRIDE

Harlequin Presents #2255
Available in June

This tycoon has met his match, and he's decided he *has* to have her...*whatever* that takes!

Pick up a Harlequin Presents® novel and you will enter a world of spine-tingling passion and provocative, tantalizing romance!

Available wherever Harlequin books are sold.

HARLEQUIN®
Makes any time special ®

Coming Next Month

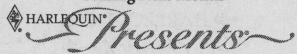

HARLEQUIN *Presents*

THE BEST HAS JUST GOTTEN BETTER!

#2253 THE ARRANGED MARRIAGE Emma Darcy

Alex King is the eldest grandson of a prestigious family—and it's his duty to expand the King empire. He must find a bride and then father a son. Alex thinks he's made the right choice, so why is his grandmother so eager to change his mind?

#2254 THE SHEIKH'S CHOSEN WIFE Michelle Reid

Leona misses her arrogant, passionate husband, Sheikh Hassan ben Al-Qadim, very much. She'd left him after she'd been unable to give him the heir he needed. But a year later Hassan tricks her into returning....

#2255 THE GREEK TYCOON'S BRIDE Helen Brooks

Andreas Karydis had women falling at his feet, so Sophy was determined not be another notch in his bedpost. But he doesn't want her as his mistress—he wants her as his English bride!

#2256 THE MISTRESS SCANDAL Kim Lawrence

Ally didn't regret her one night of passion with Gabe MacAllister and had never forgotten it. She was reminded every time she looked at her baby son. Then three years later, Ally is stunned to discover that Gabe is the brother of her sister's new fiancé!

#2257 EXPECTING HIS BABY Sandra Field

Lise knew all about ruthless airline tycoon Judd Harwood—but he needed a nanny for his daughter, Emmy, and against her better judgment Lise took the job. She never intended to spend a night of blazing passion in his bed!

#2258 THE PLAYBOY'S PROPOSAL Amanda Browning

Joel Kendrick was the sexiest man Kathryn had ever met. Never one to refuse a challenge, she flirted back when Joel flirted with her! But flirting turned to desire on Joel's part—and true love on Kathryn's....

HPCNM0502